W9-ACM-490

THE HERO POSE

THE HERO POSE

GLEN EBISCH

FIVE STAR
A part of Gale, Cengage Learning

GALE
CENGAGE Learning·

Detroit • New York • San Francisco • New Haven, Conn • Waterville, Maine • London

GALE
CENGAGE Learning·

LIBRARY OF CONGRESS CATALOGING-IN-PUBLICATION DATA

Ebisch, Glen Albert, 1946–
   The hero pose / Glen Ebisch. — First edition.
      pages cm
   ISBN-13: 978-1-4328-2680-2 (hardcover)
   ISBN-10: 1-4328-2680-8 (hardcover)
   1. Retired military personnel—Psychology—Fiction. 2. Yoga—Study and teaching—Fiction. 3. Missing persons—Investigation—Fiction. 4. Physicians—Crimes against—Fiction. 5. Psychological fiction. I. Title.
   PS3605.B57H47 2013
   813'.6—dc23   2012046486

First Edition. First Printing: April 2013
Find us on Facebook– https://www.facebook.com/FiveStarCengage
Visit our website– http://www.gale.cengage.com/fivestar/
Contact Five Star™ Publishing at FiveStar@cengage.com

Printed in Mexico
1 2 3 4 5 6 7 17 16 15 14 13

THE HERO POSE

CHAPTER 1

I pushed the switch and watched the bag of the vacuum expand like the lungs of some strange creature suddenly brought to life. The high-pitched sound of the motor filled the air, and my mind gently relaxed into the soothing white noise. I went back and forth methodically across the floor, making furrows in the pile like a farmer plowing a field. When I was finished going the long way, I went in the opposite direction until I had a checkerboard effect. I found the familiar pattern soothing and figured it was also effective. Somewhere I had read that you had to work the nap both ways in order to get a carpet really clean.

Lots of yoga studios don't worry much about cleanliness. I make a point of it. The sticky mats get cleaned once a week and the blankets once a month—no lingering smells of year-old perfume or flowery deodorant for me. I even take the covers off the eye bags and wash them every other week. No one wants to catch an infection in her third eye while meditating.

I do all of this not just for the results, but because I find the routine comforting. Some people might say that I seek out the little jobs in order to fill up time—to prevent my mind from wandering to other, less pleasant things. I prefer to think that it helps me live mindfully in the moment like the sages recommend, not dwelling on the past or worrying about the future.

"My name is Alison Randall, and I live in the present," I repeated to myself like a personal mantra.

As I vacuumed the row closest to the front of the studio I

looked out the window, being careful to really see what was actually there and not drift off down the river of free association. I'm on the third floor of a small office building. It gives me an expansive view across Route 1 and out over the tidal marsh, only stopping at the row of what look like toy houses along the edge of the ocean about a mile away. It was a sunny day in late September. From where I stood, the Atlantic was a narrow strip of steel blue defining the horizon off the coast of southern Maine, off the town of Cornwall, to be exact.

Later in the day I would walk on the beach that was invisible from here, briskly going three miles in one direction, focusing on the feeling of the sand moving under my feet with each step. Then, turning around, I would meticulously place my feet back in the same footprints and make my return. According to tradition, some enlightened ones left no footprints in the sand at all. I wasn't quite up to that. But on a more practical note, being tired by the end of the day would help me sleep. That's important to me.

Damn, I thought, pulling myself violently back from the future to the present, then remembering, too late, that I should be more forgiving of myself. It's hard not to live in the future. Even harder, for me, is not to live in the past.

A hand came down lightly on my shoulder. Before the sensation fully registered, I spun around, setting off a sharp flash of pain in my damaged hip. My left hand automatically grabbed my assailant's arm and my right hand formed a hard fist that drove toward where I estimated his midsection to be. An instant before I would have made contact, I saw Lauren's pale face, her eyes staring wide with terror. Her expression registered just in time. I checked my motion, stumbling forward and brushing her with my shoulder. She gave a quick scream and tumbled back hard onto the carpet. She sat there looking up at me, making no attempt to get to her feet.

I turned off the vacuum, and took a deep breath to center myself. When my heart rate had returned closer to normal, I reached down and offered her my hand. She stared at it for a while, as if wondering whether it was some kind of lethal device, not a human appendage at all. Finally she gambled and put her hand in mine. I gently helped her to her feet. She backed away a couple of steps, then stood very still as if afraid of provoking me. I was the friendly dog that had suddenly turned and snapped at her. She was afraid and her feelings were hurt. She wasn't sure whether I had changed permanently into a threatening creature or whether that had been merely a momentary aberration.

Lauren Malcolm was in her early thirties but looked younger due to being slender and petite, and also because she had a wide-eyed expression that made her appear naïve and innocent. I didn't know if that was really true of her personality or just a physiological quirk. She was a student at my yoga center. I'd introduced myself to her when she started taking classes two months ago. Since then I'd seen her in the studio several times, although she practiced with one of the other teachers.

"I startle easily," I said. "You shouldn't have surprised me."

"I didn't mean to, Ali. The vacuum was on. I called your name, but you didn't hear me."

"Then you should have waited. I would have seen you eventually."

"I have to talk to you. I need your help."

I frowned. "I don't do that."

"Do what?"

"Help people."

She stared at me incredulously with her wide eyes, as if I had announced that I had a spare head that I kept in a hatbox in my bedroom closet.

"You don't? Isn't that sort of . . . selfish?" she blurted out.

Some people would find her directness charming. I had heard that Lauren was a realtor, and perhaps her clients considered her apparent openness to be reassuring. After all, someone who revealed her emotions so easily wouldn't possibly attempt to deceive anyone, would she? I didn't know the answer to that, and didn't intend to find out.

"No, it isn't selfish," I said, "because I don't expect others to help me. I don't mistreat people, I simply avoid getting involved in their lives." I paused, not sure how much to try to explain myself. After all, even explanations are a form of involvement. A way of exposing yourself to others. I kept it short. "I live my own life. I don't have any energy left over for others."

"But you're the only one I know who can help me."

"Why?"

"My boyfriend has disappeared."

I frowned at her non-responsive answer but played along.

"How do you know?"

She gaped at me as if I weren't making sense.

"People choose to go away all the time. They hit the road, take a hike, vamoose, make tracks, follow their bliss, so just because you don't know where he's gone doesn't mean that he's disappeared."

She shook her head. "It's not just me. No one knows where he is."

"Why not go to the police?"

"They think maybe he committed suicide."

"So he's dead, not disappeared?"

"Can't we sit down and talk about this?" Lauren asked, desperately glancing over her shoulder in the direction of my small front office.

I didn't budge. Every bad journey begins with the first step.

"So why did you come to me?"

She sighed. "Because I've heard that you were an M.P. in Iraq."

"This isn't Iraq, and we're not in the military," I pointed out.

"And you're the only woman I know who's been shot."

I was tempted to shake my head to see if I could get her disjointed comments to line up in some kind of order.

"How do you know I was shot?"

"It gets around. People talk. Plus anyone can see that you've got a limp."

And here I'd figured it was hardly noticeable anymore.

"I wasn't shot, I was hit by shrapnel. And what does any of this have to do with finding your dead or missing boyfriend?"

"He was married—sort of—to somebody else. Only another woman is going to take my problem seriously."

I sighed. Her first good answer so far.

"Let's go into my office," I said.

CHAPTER 2

Calling my office an office is a gross misuse of the word. Situated off the lobby, where the students sit on facing benches lined up along the two walls to remove their shoes, it's more in the nature of a grotto. A dark, windowless space with a desk where my computer resides, a beast I am slowly training to develop a mailing list that will eventually generate more business in one of my future lifetimes. Next to the computer is a phone with an answering machine that fortunately has been ringing slightly more often lately. There are two chairs and a set of shelves that holds my small collection of yoga and meditation books. I sat in the marginally more comfortable chair behind the desk, while Lauren perched on the edge of the cheap green plastic model that a previous renter had generously left behind.

"Your missing boyfriend is married?" I asked.

"But separated," she added quickly. "He's getting a divorce, but it won't be final for about another four months."

I guessed she pretended to estimate in order to save her pride. I was willing to bet that, if pressed, she could tell me down to the day, hour, and minute when the divorce would come through. I would have asked, but I didn't want to embarrass her.

"We've been going out for six months. Once his divorce is final, we're going to get married."

I kept a neutral expression. I am a woman, after all, despite my limitations. A man's face would have given a skeptical twitch at this point in the story, revealing his belief in the universal gullibility of women when it comes to love. Having been on the receiving side of that twitch, I wasn't comfortable dishing it out.

"So why do the police think your boyfriend could be dead?"

"They found his car parked by the beach. They think . . . they think that maybe he walked into the ocean."

I liked that expression. Going for a stroll out into the ocean was an oddly liberating image; it got me wondering how many people chose that particular method of suicide. I'd heard that the Jains, a relatively small religious group in India, sometimes practice it, although they generally prefer self-starvation. Of course, they believe it's only appropriate for those who have reached the right point of spiritual development. I doubted that Lauren's boyfriend was a Jain.

Off the coast of Maine the water in September would still be fairly warm. Your body wouldn't rapidly become paralyzed. A picture came to me of a man walking and walking until the water was over his head, then continuing to walk along the ocean bottom. But wouldn't your body naturally float? And what if you could swim? Did you keep swimming toward the horizon until exhausted, then just sink? Of course, there have been nights when the full moon has thrown an inviting snow-white path across the ocean's surface that I've been tempted to travel. I forced my mind back to the present.

"When did this happen?"

"Friday. It was in the newspaper," Lauren said in a tone that accused me of not following current events.

"I don't read the newspaper."

"And you don't teach the Saturday or Sunday classes, so I couldn't reach you here," Lauren said sharply, as if I were being lax. "I wanted to call you over the weekend, but your phone number is unlisted. And when I took Karen's class on Saturday, she said that you didn't let people give out your personal number."

13

Karen was one of my teachers. Neither she nor Julie, my other employee, would be foolish enough to give out my cell number. They know I value my privacy.

"You could have left a message on the phone here. I check the voicemail from home once in a while." She opened her mouth to respond. But before she could complain some more about my irresponsible lifestyle, I asked, "Was your boyfriend depressed?"

I could see her start to deny it, then she paused. "He was worried about his two sons growing up without a father in the home. I think he was also concerned about whether the divorce would have an effect on his practice."

"His practice?"

"He's a medical doctor down at the Cornwall emergency care center. Maybe you know him, Dr. Jim Schianno?"

I shook my head, but that was a lie. I just didn't want to get into a long discussion of the guy with Lauren. I had met Dr. Jim, as he had asked me to call him, about two months ago. This first-name business is phony friendliness in my opinion. Priests and doctors should stick with their last names so the lines of authority remain clear. Everyone knows that the moment you disagree with them rank will quickly reassert itself, so why start off as if it were anything other than a power relationship?

I'd gone in to see Dr. Jim to have a piece of shrapnel removed that was starting to break through the skin. The big pieces that went deep into muscle tissue had been taken out shortly after the attack, but there were lots of smaller shards left behind. The docs said that it would do less damage to leave them there than to dig around looking. They assured me that eventually most of them would work their way to the surface on their own—little metallic mementos of my vacation in Iraq. Possibly I could have dug this one out myself. I've done it in the past. But it felt like a bigger piece than I wanted to pull out using a hand mirror and a pair of eyebrow tweezers. Dr. Jim had silently studied my left hip, which looks like someone had ravaged it with a dull peeling knife.

"That must have been very painful when it happened."

"Only after the shock wore off."

"How long did that take?"

"It hasn't yet."

To give him credit, Dr. Jim took my answer as a sign that I didn't want to chat.

"Probably you should see a surgeon about this. Technically it's a hospital outpatient procedure."

I began to get dressed.

"I guess I can take care of it myself," I said.

He placed a firm hand on my arm.

"I'll do it."

He walked over to the cabinet and removed a vial.

"What's that for?"

"An injection of local anesthetic."

"Skip it."

"I'll have to cut to get it all out."

I shrugged.

"This might hurt."

"I'm sure it will."

When he was done and taping a piece of gauze over the wound, he rolled his stool around where he could see my face.

"You're not a flincher."

"What's that?"

"Most people pull away from the scalpel at the last minute because they anticipate the pain. You didn't move."

"I expect pain. If I weren't willing to accept it, I wouldn't be here."

He cleared his throat slowly, debating with himself whether

to take on an even more unpleasant job than cutting through my skin.

"Have you gotten any counseling?"

"Sure. I had a couple of meetings with an army shrink just before I got out."

"What did he say?"

"He told me to think positively."

Dr. Jim gave me a bleak smile.

"Are you seeing a counselor now?"

"I've got a friend."

"Does he have professional training?"

"He's a Reiki Master."

To his credit, Dr. Jim remained expressionless.

"Does he help you?"

I paused for a moment. That was a question I couldn't remember ever having asked myself. I kept seeing Izzy because I enjoyed our conversations, but it had never occurred to me to ask whether our association was doing me any good.

"Yes. I think he does," I answered, surprising myself.

Dr. Jim nodded.

"Whatever works," he said and gave me a crooked smile.

I tried to picture Dr. Jim walking out into the ocean with that same bemused smile on his face, but couldn't quite bring it into focus. I turned my attention back to Lauren.

"How long has the car been there?"

"The police aren't sure. I talked to his nurse. She said that he left work at five o'clock on Thursday. He was supposed to be at my place at six-thirty. He always comes to my place on Tuesday, Thursday, and Sunday," she announced proudly, as if that were the temporal equivalent of a wedding ring.

"Does he stay overnight?"

"Unless he's got something important going on at work first thing in the morning."

He was in family practice, not a surgeon, I thought. What kind of early morning work did he have? Maybe he just liked to be alone or with someone else.

"When he didn't show up on Thursday night," Lauren went on, "I figured maybe something had come up at the hospital or with his kids, although I was a little surprised that he hadn't called. He's always been good about letting me know if he can't make it. I waited until about ten, then I tried to call him on his cell phone, but got no answer. That's when I started to get concerned."

Frantic with worry, anger, and fear of rejection was more like it, I guessed.

"I still couldn't get through to him at his apartment on Friday morning, so I called the practice when it opened. His nurse told me he hadn't come in yet, and he had patients waiting. She had tried his apartment, too, and gotten no answer. She said his wife had no idea where he was either. Maggie Croyson, that's his nurse's name, said she had tried calling every place she could think of with no success."

"Did she know about you and Dr. Jim?"

Lauren nodded.

"But she didn't call to see if he was with you when he didn't show up at work?"

"Jim went out with her briefly after leaving his wife and before he met me. I think she's still a little jealous and doesn't like to talk to me."

I nodded.

"After I told her that he hadn't shown up the night before, she got really worried and called the police. At first they didn't want to do anything because he hadn't been missing very long, but Maggie insisted that he always came to work, so something serious must have happened."

"What did the police do?"

"They went to his apartment. He wasn't there. It didn't look as though he had been there overnight, and his car was missing. They alerted their patrol officers to keep an eye out for it. That's how they found his car."

"Where was it?"

"On a street that ends at the beach on Turtle Island."

Turtle Island was part of Cornwall, connected by a short causeway that you'd miss if you blinked. Anyone with a halfway decent arm could toss a stone from the mainland to the island. There were maybe thirty houses, most belonged to families that had bought in a couple of generations ago and passed the places on. Today even the dumpiest of them was worth well over half a million. There were few year-round residents. Since it was now after Labor Day, the island would be mostly deserted except on weekends, when folks might come up from Boston or down from Portland to eke out a few last days of summer.

"Do you know if the police found anything that suggested violence?"

Lauren shook her head. "I finally got up my nerve and called Jim's wife. She told me that the car was locked. They had to get a locksmith to open it. But there was no blood or anything."

Would someone about to commit suicide lock his car? I wondered. I remembered one soldier who carefully made up his bed and secured his footlocker before going out behind the barracks and blowing his head off with his M16. But he was known to be an obsessive-compulsive. I could see Dr. Jim closing his car door before taking a watery walk, but locking it was more questionable. I remembered having it drilled into me that everything a suicide does just before committing the act has significance; nobody performs meaningless acts during their last moments. The trick was figuring out what that meaning might be.

Lauren had lost all of her earlier energy and was slumped

over in the chair, staring at the floor. Even her hair seemed to have lost its body and hung limply across her face.

"What do you think happened to him?" I asked to keep her focused.

Her head came up halfway and she glanced at me like a whipped puppy. I didn't know which she needed more, a warm hug or a bracing slap on the face. She wasn't getting either one from me. Both were too intimate.

"I was kind of pressuring him to set a date for when we'd get married. And he was worrying about paying alimony and child support. Maybe he just couldn't take it any more."

"And did what?" I asked.

"I hope he just went somewhere to think about things," she said softly.

Drove down to the beach, left his car, and then ran away. I considered it. That would be enough to plant the suspicion of suicide in the minds of the cops and slow down any enthusiasm for a search. It would also suggest that he'd had some help—at least a ride out of there. But was this a little vacation from responsibility, or was Dr. Jim under enough pressure that he'd give up a good profession and start all over again somewhere else just to avoid a bitter wife and an insistent girlfriend?

Of course there was a third alternative.

"Can you think of any reason why he might have gone to Turtle Island to meet someone?"

Her eyes flashed and her spine suddenly straightened. "You mean a woman?"

I shrugged.

"Jim wouldn't cheat on me."

I nodded. His wife and nurse Maggie had probably already sung that old country tune.

"Did Dr. Jim do drugs?"

"No. Why do you ask?"

"Some doctors do. And Turtle Island is a nice quiet spot for that kind of transaction."

She shook her head until her hair swirled. "Jim was a responsible man and a good doctor."

"Have you noticed any changes in him recently?"

"He's been a little down for a while, but like I said, I figured that was just because of the arguments with his wife over the divorce."

"Any worse most recently?"

"On Tuesday when he came over he was really distracted."

"Did he give you any idea what was bothering him?"

"He didn't want to talk about it. You know how men are."

I didn't actually, and neither did she.

I steepled my fingers and sat staring at them as if lost in thought about Dr. Jim's mysterious disappearance. Actually I was trying to figure out how to tell Lauren that there was nothing I could do for her. If Jim had committed suicide, that was his own decision, one I could possibly respect, but do nothing about. If an enraged girlfriend or a drug dealer had murdered him that night, then it was a police matter. If he'd done a runner, I was sure he'd had his reasons. From our brief acquaintance, I'd liked him more than I liked Lauren, so I wasn't about to drag him back to her happy love nest.

"Will you help me?" she asked, clasping her hands and stretching out her arms in front of her in a classic pleading posture. I wondered if she'd ever acted in bad amateur theatre.

"Look, Lauren—"

She grabbed for the small purse that hung over her shoulder.

"I can pay you for your time. I have plenty of money saved up."

"No," I said, waving a hand in the air, pushing the thought away.

She smiled and reached out, touching my hand. It took all

my self-control not to pull back. Instead I gradually liberated my hand and returned it to the safety of my lap.

"I knew you wouldn't take money. I knew you were a good person."

"I'm not," I said, shocked almost speechless by the thought. "Let the police do their job. They'll find out whatever there is to discover."

Her outstretched arms twisted into a reasonable facsimile of the Eagle Arm posture as she continued squeezing her hands in front of her face.

"Whatever they find out, the police won't tell me anything. I'm just the other woman. They'll tell his wife. She's passed along a few things to me so far, but I can't keep calling her. She was so cool and distant. It made me uncomfortable. That means I won't know what's happening. I'll be left in the dark."

She was right. She had no legal standing, and the police, generally being rather traditional in their thinking, would not be much inclined to share information with her. In my own different way, I knew what that felt like.

"I'll talk to the police and see what I can find out," I said. "But that's all I'll promise."

She jumped to her feet and opened her arms, clearly planning to put them around me, a move that would have been hard to gracefully avoid in such a confined space. But just then the door opened, stopping Lauren in her tracks, so I didn't have to use force to avoid her show of affection.

CHAPTER 3

Julie and Karen walked into the lobby. As soon as they saw Lauren and me standing in the office doorway facing each other as if at the end of a melodramatic scene in a soap opera, they stopped talking and hesitated as if unsure whether they were intruding. Lauren's expression when she turned to face them was so forlorn it begged for someone to ask what was wrong.

"Come on in, guys," I said with enthusiasm, and as quickly as I could slipped past Lauren and out into the relative freedom of the lobby.

I sounded so uncharacteristically happy to see them that they were momentarily paralyzed. I made a show of checking the time by studying my large statue of the Buddha with a clock face in his belly that I keep on a table in the lobby, a bit of kitsch I'd picked up at a tag sale when decorating the studio. It was three feet tall and made of heavy terra cotta. Really spiritual people were probably offended by it, but I figured it showed that I have a sense of humor. Something most people seem not to believe.

"Almost time to get ready for class," I announced cheerfully, sounding manic even to myself.

"Right," Julie said, recovering first. Only a couple of years out of college, she was almost as tall as my five-ten, but with more generous curves and a wholesome prettiness that I lacked.

She flashed a giant smile in the direction of Lauren and me, which didn't mean anything because Julie was that way with everybody. She went into the large classroom to begin stretching. Whatever private psychodrama was going on, she wanted no part of it.

Dressed in her tight fitting yoga togs, Julie Sawyer could provoke envy in most women and lust in the occasional male who took classes. She offset both by being politely cheerful and friendly. A mask that kept her students at a distance but at the same time offended no one. I'd never seen the mask slip, even when the two of us were alone. That was fine with me. Seeing people's real faces was above my pay grade.

Karen Unger, in her late thirties and more maternal than Julie, made a beeline over to us and asked Lauren if anything was wrong. Karen's large brown eyes were filled with concern. Probably most people would have described them as caring, but to me they were bovine. I could see Lauren getting ready to repeat the sad story of Dr. Jim all over again in every detail, so I quickly suggested that they go into the classroom where Karen was scheduled to teach and have their conversation in private. I breathed a sigh of relief as they walked off side by side. Lauren usually took classes with Karen, and I hoped that Karen, with her gentle disposition and aura of concern, could handle whatever soul baring remained to be done.

I went back into the cave and sat down. I glanced at the calendar and saw that it happened to be six months to the day since I had opened the studio. A date worth celebrating, if I believed in that sort of thing. Julie had been the first person I'd hired. I'd started by teaching five classes a week myself and hired Julie to cover the three additional classes offered. Having only one part-time employee seemed like a good way to keep costs down until the business was on its feet. Like most plans, the weakness in this one was in the planner. I discovered within a month that I couldn't teach five classes in my usual style without having a constantly aching hip. Some yoga teachers tell you what to do, then watch to see that you're doing it properly and offer advice. I think of that as the drill sergeant approach. I prefer to do the exercises right along with the student—I don't expect you to do anything I wouldn't do. I lead from the front.

I had struggled along for another month, practicing alternate nostril breathing to ease the pain until I'd practically forgotten how to breathe through both nostrils at once. By then the number of students had slowly begun to grow, and I figured that the summer months would bring even more students along with an influx of tourists. So I revised my plan. In July I cut back on the number of classes I taught and hired Karen.

I'd had a few doubts as to her skills at first because she was short and rather pear-shaped, hardly the slender yogic ideal. After sitting in on a couple of her classes, however, I realized that she was extremely strong and flexible, an inspiration to all students with larger bodies. Although she was only in her late thirties, maybe ten years older than I am, there was something solid and nurturing about Karen that seemed to attract the young mothers and the singles with problems. Since Julie appealed to the young and the vigorous, I was left with the ragtag remainder, composed mostly of the eccentric, the physically injured, and the old. That suited me just fine because they were so caught up in their own lives, they didn't ask about mine.

One exception was Jack Branson, a police detective lieutenant here in Cornwall who'd been taking classes with me for the last two months. His back had gotten racked up when he was rear ended by a drunk while assisting an officer at a routine traffic stop. A nurse down at York Hospital, where he was doing rehab, had suggested that yoga might help him regain flexibility. Unlike some men I've had in class, he took it seriously, but I could tell by his attempts to initiate small talk that his interest in yoga extended to the teacher. A couple of inches taller than I am and not bad looking in a soulful sort of way, he seemed like a smart, sensitive guy who would be fun to know. In another lifetime I might have been interested. After my promise to Lauren, I was more interested in him as a source of information.

I felt the vibration of feet coming up the stairs. In a few minutes the lobby would be crowded with women chattering noisily while taking off their shoes in preparation for the two classes. Monday is the busiest morning, as everyone tries to start the week off right. If I stayed in the office, someone was bound to pop into the doorway and try to strike up a conversation. I'd pretty much depleted my store of small talk for the day with Lauren, so I stuck my head in Julie's room and told her to lock up when she left because I was going out. Then I rushed down the stairs, going against the tide of women heading to class, calling out a couple of random "hi's" and "how're you doin's" to keep them sweet, while being careful not to make eye contact. When I reached the parking lot, I took a deep breath and looked around me, savoring the moment of aloneness, then I walked over to my car. I tried to be present in the moment, I walked slowly, feeling my foot making complete contact with the asphalt on each step.

My green Mazda sparkled in the mid-morning sun. It should. I'd purchased it new about eight months ago when I'd first moved down to Cornwall. It was the first car I'd ever owned.

At home and in college I'd had the use of one of the family cars. My father liked cars, so there were always three or four around. My two older brothers were each given their own as soon as they got their licenses. I preferred to borrow. By then I wasn't into taking gifts from Dad. In the Army I'd never needed a car. When stationed stateside, I'd found there were always folks who couldn't live without their own set of wheels, and those of us who were single tended to go places together. Overseas you either signed something out from the motor pool or took public transport.

But when I'd finished my speedy three weeks of rehab at Bethesda, I'd suddenly found myself out of the Army and out of the hospital on the same day. I stood on the street with my duffel bag over my shoulder and realized that I had nowhere to go and no way to get there. I considered taking a taxi to the bus depot and hopping a Greyhound to anywhere out west, but the thought of sitting on a bus filled with other people made my skin crawl. I'd seen too much of other people in the last few years.

Instead I took a taxi to the nearest rental car agency that would let me take a vehicle out of state. Then I made the first left turn out of the parking lot and began to drive. When I found I was heading north, I figured that was as good a direction as any other. How far north I would have gone is anyone's guess—maybe mine would have been the first Taurus at the North Pole—but a deer with a suicide wish just north of Brunswick, Maine, took out my windshield and that's how I discovered the Savasana Retreat Center.

A bubbly young woman who gave me a ride there to use the phone said that Savasana was the Sanskrit word for relaxation and that for a moderate fee and the performance of daily chores I could stay and study yoga. I liked the idea of relaxation, so I had my rental car towed away and decided to hang around for a while. Later, when I had settled in there and started taking yoga classes, I found out that Savasana referred specifically to the posture that was taken at the end of a session, lying on your back with your arms beside you, mentally assimilating all that you had just experienced. Even later, I discovered this was called the Corpse pose. I liked that even better. I decided the Ali Randall I was had died right along with that deer by the side of the road, and whoever came out of the Savasana Retreat Center living in her body would be a different person.

That new person, appearing eighteen months later with a

recently minted certificate qualifying her as a yoga teacher, had rented another car and headed south until the coast went from rocky to sandy. She had eventually ended up in Cornwall, still without a car to her name, so that's why I'd finally bought this one when I decided to stop moving.

I started the engine and pulled out of the small strip mall where my studio is located. I took a left and went through the center of town, which is three blocks of small shops—most catering to the tourist trade—a couple of banks, two liquor stores, and three pizzerias. I made another left at the light. A half-mile farther and I made a final left at a small sign that said "Town Buildings." A hundred yards farther along, the road opened up to reveal a parking lot and three recently constructed structures: a town hall, a senior citizen center, and a police station. I'd come to suspect all three of them had been purposely hidden away so tourists couldn't easily discover them. No sense in wasting taxpayer money on transients.

I parked in front of the police station and walked through the double doors. I stood politely at the counter until the desk sergeant, who was staring at the computer screen as if it were a crystal ball, noticed me.

"Can I help you?"

"I'd like to see Lieutenant Branson."

"Is he expecting you?"

I shook my head.

"I'll see if he's available," he said, furrowing his brow as if I had a better chance of getting an audience with the pope.

Before the sergeant could even get to his feet, Jack appeared in the nearest doorway looking solemn as always. He has the large eyes and sharp features of someone who's spent too much time in the desert talking to God.

"Alison," he said. A smile of pleasure lit up his face like sun through the clouds. "I thought I heard your voice. Come on in."

The sergeant raised his eyebrows and buzzed open a gate to my left. I felt guilty because I knew my reality wouldn't meet Jack's high expectations. He stuck out his hand, and I shook it as if we hadn't seen each other only two days before. He ushered me into his office. The white walls were made blindingly bright by the eastern sun pouring through the two windows behind his desk. It was a more cheerful room than I was familiar with from most military police stations, where the colors tended toward pea-soup green. He settled behind his desk and gestured for me to take one of the two seats in front.

"How can I help you?" he asked with a smile.

I wished I had been interrupting something important, so I could succinctly ask and he could curtly answer my questions. All this cheerful goodwill would be harder to navigate.

"Lauren Malcolm is one of my students, and she asked me if I would look into the disappearance of her friend, Jim Schianno," I said, getting right to the point, so he wouldn't mistake this for a social call.

" 'Look into'?" Jack said. The smile had faded a bit when he realized this wasn't a social call, but I was relieved to see that he was still looking more amused than angry.

"Not in the sense of investigate," I said quickly, as if that were beyond the realm of thought, "but she's concerned about her friend and afraid that the police won't share any information with her because she isn't family."

He paused for a moment to consider my proposal. "So your role would be that of a communicator. You would pass along whatever we were willing to tell her."

"Exactly."

"She asked you to do this because of your criminal justice background?"

Somehow Jack had known from the first about my career as an M.P. I dimly recalled having mentioned it once to a student

28

who inquired about my limp, and it had spread around town like ripples across a small pond. Since then I'd become much more cautious in what I volunteered about myself. Evasiveness was now my middle name.

I shrugged. "I guess she thought I'd be more comfortable talking to the police than a plain civilian and better able to understand what you had to say."

"Well, what I can tell you isn't very technical, and she probably knows it all already from the papers and town gossip. We found his car at the end of Monroe Street down by Turtle Island. There were no signs of foul play, but we also haven't found any signs of the doc. His credit cards haven't been used, and there's been no activity on his bank accounts. Nobody we've contacted has seen the doc since a neighbor spotted him leaving his apartment at about seven o'clock on Thursday night."

"So he came home from work, then went out again at seven. And his car was found at Turtle Island the next morning. It was locked, right?"

Jack raised an eyebrow. "So that got out, too?"

I nodded. "Lauren seems to think that he might have needed to get away because of the stress of his divorce."

"Frankly, I've seen weddings that were more stressful. From what I've heard, Dr. Jim and his wife seemed to be working things out in a pretty amicable way."

I wondered to myself if he had exaggerated the horrors of home life in order to make Lauren feel more secure.

"Any chance that he met up with some unsavory characters?"

Jack shook his head. "It's always possible. But Turtle Island isn't exactly a hotbed of crime, and as far as we know he wasn't into drugs, gambling, or any illegal activities."

"Any reason he would take a stroll into the sea?"

"His wife said that he'd been very agitated for the last week or so, but she had no idea why. And she didn't think he was the type to commit suicide."

"Is there a type?" I asked. "Wouldn't anyone do it under the right circumstances?"

Jack gave me a long, concerned look. "The doc's life didn't seem that tough to me, but you never know what's going on inside someone's head."

"Where would his body wash up if it was a suicide?"

"If he went in right off the shore and with normal currents like we're having now, he'd probably travel no more than ten miles down the coast, no farther than York. But it could be as much as a week before he came close enough to shore to be spotted. And, of course, some floaters are never found. The ocean is a busy and unpredictable place."

"So it's possible we'll never know for sure whether he's dead or took off for parts unknown?"

Jack agreed.

I didn't think that would make Lauren happy. Most people think bad news is better than uncertainty because it brings closure. In my opinion, closure is overrated. At least uncertainty leaves open the possibility of a happy result.

"Dr. Jim had at least two relationships in the months since he left his wife. I'd be willing to bet that there were others before that," I said.

Jack nodded. "This goes back to before your time, but there were a few stories that went around suggesting the good doctor had quite a bedside manner."

"Do you have any details?"

"Nothing specific."

"Would you mind if I talked to his wife myself? I'd like to get her perspective on things. It might help give Lauren a fuller sense of the situation."

"If Mrs. Schianno is willing, I won't stand in your way."

"Thanks," I said and started to stand.

Jack stood up as well. "I'm a little surprised that you wanted to get involved in this." He paused as if searching for the right words. "You don't strike me as the naturally curious type."

"I have my reasons this time."

He nodded, accepting the fact that I wasn't going to tell him more.

"Maybe we could get together for a drink and to talk about other things."

I shook my head. "I don't drink."

"I see."

"I gave it up for Lent."

"It isn't Lent."

"It's always Lent," I said, struggling to my feet.

"Maybe a cup of coffee, then?"

"Caffeine makes me nervous."

"I don't think it's the caffeine that makes you nervous," he said solemnly.

I didn't have a quick comeback for that, so I turned to head for the door. He strode across the room quickly and opened it for me.

"Thanks for stopping by, Alison," he said, putting a gentle hand on my shoulder as if soothing a restless horse.

I turned and stared into his brown, sad eyes and tried to smile. By the expression on his face and the speed with which he removed his hand, I think it must have come out more as a grimace.

CHAPTER 4

People can be a surprise sometimes. I don't get surprised much because I've gotten out of the habit of developing expectations. I've reached the point where I take people as they are in the moment and don't assume their behavior will be the same in the next hour, the next day, or the next week. I observe people like watching the dice roll, curious to see what will turn up, and not making predictions.

But I'll admit that I had anticipated Dianne Schianno, Dr. Jim's wife, would be less than thrilled to meet with me. After all, I was working for her husband's girlfriend, someone whom Mrs. Schianno might reasonably perceive as a home wrecker. However, she listened on the phone without interruption as I gave the same rather thin explanation for what I was doing that I'd given to Jack, and then politely invited me to come over to see her later that morning.

The Schiannos lived about five miles west of Cornwall in an area rich with pine forests and rolling hills. Their house was a rambling, wood-shingled ranch set in the middle of a large lawn that ran down to the road in front and ended in a dense line of tall pines in back. It was an open, sunny space, good for raising plants and children.

The woman who answered the door was petite, pretty, and in her early forties. Her hair was medium length and one of those colors between brown and blond that women's hair seems to become either by nature or intention as they approach middle age. She opened the door and invited me in with a pleasant enough smile, although I thought I detected some wariness in her eyes. Since I always see that in people's eyes, I discounted it.

We moved down a short hall into a family room on the left. There was a large sectional sofa and two chairs. Everything seemed to be of good quality but had the worn appearance that comes with hard family use. The giant television in the corner of the room looked new. I ignored her offer of a place on the sofa and sat in one of the chairs. Having arms on a chair helps me get out of it more easily when the hip gets balky.

Dianne settled onto the sofa, sitting forward on the edge of the cushion with both feet planted on the floor. For most people that would have been an awkward posture, but she seemed to relax into it. Being alert and at the same time comfortable must have come naturally to her.

"I'm sorry about your husband," I began.

"So am I," she said.

We both paused for a moment as if considering the ambiguity of our comments. Were we sorry he was dead, assuming he was? Or were we sorry that he had chosen to disappear, if he had? Or were we just sorry that he had left his family for another woman?

"The boys are both at school," she continued. "I couldn't see any point in keeping them home when the police have no idea whether they'll ever know more than they do right now. A set routine is important to children."

"For adults, too," I said.

She frowned. "For adults it's a blessing and a curse. We like the security that comes with predictability, but we're quickly bored by the routine. Then we try to break out, and when things begin to go badly, we come running back home."

There was some truth in that. Soldiers in a combat zone talk endlessly about what they'll do when they get back home, but once the initial novelty of home wears off, they miss the excitement and camaraderie they left behind, forgetting about the periods of mind-numbing terror that went along with it.

"Was that what your husband did? Were his extramarital adventures little breaks from the routine followed by his returning home for forgiveness?"

I tried to make my tone gentle, but people tell me that even at its sweetest, my voice cracks like a whip. Dianne didn't flinch or seem shocked. I gave her credit for that.

"It wasn't quite so simple—for either one of us."

"Why not?"

Dianne stared at my face. "What happened to your nose?" she asked.

"What about it?"

"Obviously it was broken at some time in the past. Was it done by a man?"

"A boy, actually," I said.

I reached up and touched it, not able to help myself. It had a noticeable bump in the middle and turned slightly to the left. Whenever I looked in the mirror, the asymmetry made it hard for me to see my face as a whole. I always seemed to be looking at one side or the other, as if it were two faces fused into one like a not very imaginative Picasso.

"A youthful romance gone sour?" she asked me.

I shook my head. "I have two older brothers. We were playing basketball in the driveway at home. I guess I was thirteen or so. They must have been fifteen and sixteen."

"So it was an accident?" Dianne asked, sounding disappointed.

If it hadn't seemed to matter to her so much, I might have said that it was and left it at that. There were times when I pretended to myself that it was an accident, even though I knew otherwise. But there was something in the way she asked, not so much a plea for sympathy as a desire to establish a connection. I wasn't sure I wanted one, but I sensed it was the only way I'd get any information from her.

"My brothers take after my father. They're short and heavy-set. I take after my mother. By the time I was thirteen, I was taller than either one of them. I was also a better basketball player."

"They didn't like that," she said.

"Not much. What boy likes being shown up by a girl, especially his younger sister?"

Dianne nodded.

"So it was summer and we were playing in the driveway. My older brother, Tim, had missed his shot and I was under the basket getting ready for the rebound. He'd always been taller than I was, but I'd just had a recent growth spurt and passed him. As I was looking up to catch the ball coming off the back-board, he jumped as high in the air as he could and brought his elbow down on my face. I felt a snap, blacked out for a minute, and the next thing I knew I was down on my knees with blood pouring from my nose onto the asphalt. Timmy was standing over me screaming that he'd just been going for the ball, and it was all an accident."

"What happened?"

"I got to my feet and tried to beat the crap out of Timmy even though he must have outweighed me by thirty pounds. I had him under me, pounding his head up and down on the driveway when my brother Phil pulled me off. By then Tim was hysterical and covered with my blood and snot. Phil's always had the coolest head of the three of us. He got me inside and put a wet towel on my face."

"Were there any adults at home?"

"A housekeeper. But she was out shopping."

"What about your parents?"

"My mother was already gone by then. She left us when I was a little over a year old. My father's a lawyer. He was working on a big case at the time and hardly ever came home from Boston. My brothers stuffed cotton up my nose and put ice packs on the back of my neck. Eventually the bleeding stopped. Two days later though, my eyes looked like a raccoon's, and my nose was twice its normal size."

"You should have been taken to a doctor."

"My brothers were afraid my father would find out about it. He had these periodic bouts of guilt over leaving us at home unsupervised. If he discovered what had happened to me, my brothers were afraid he'd move us closer to the city so he could be home with us every night."

"Why did that worry your brothers?"

"Dad had high hopes for them, so when he was around, they really had to toe the line."

"Did he feel the same way about you?"

"Not so much."

"So you sat around for weeks with black eyes and a swollen nose?" Dianne asked.

"Yeah. For ten days or so, I pretty much stayed in my room during the day. My brothers brought me food and stuff to read. And we each had a television in our room, so it wasn't that bad. Fortunately, the housekeeper had this idea that teenaged girls were generally sulky and broody, so it didn't surprise her that I stopped eating meals with the rest of them and kept to myself. But I got something out of it."

"What's that?"

"Timmy's new computer. The thing I had was over five years old. My father kept promising to replace it but kept forgetting. So I made Timmy pay. Of course, six months later Dad bought him an even newer one anyway."

"Didn't your father ever notice what happened to you?" Dianne smiled. "I don't mean that it looks grotesque, but you'd expect a parent to pay more attention."

"He was busy and hardly ever around. It healed up before he spotted it."

That wasn't the exact truth, but I figured that I'd spilled my guts enough for the time being. The truth is that four months later my father was home one day and happened to come into the kitchen early while I was eating breakfast. Out of the corner of my eye I saw him staring at me like he had spotted something he didn't like. That didn't particularly surprise me since he hardly ever looked at me any other way.

"There's something different about the way you look," he said.

I got to my feet, ready to make a dash to the door. "Probably need to get my hair cut."

"No, it's something about your face."

"I'm getting older. Faces change."

He stared at me a long time then had nodded sadly. "Yes, too bad. You were a pretty little girl."

"Have you ever thought about getting it fixed?" Dianne asked, bringing me back to the present.

The army plastic surgeon who worked on the small shrapnel wounds I'd gotten to the side of my face had offered to throw in a nose job for free. He said the he could always claim I'd broken my nose when I got blown out of the Humvee. I'd given it some serious thought, but then a lieutenant I met in rehab told me that if I got my nose fixed, I'd be drop-dead gorgeous. I figured he was telling me the truth because, being gay, he didn't have any ulterior motives. I decided to give the surgery a pass.

"No," I told Dianne. "I'm satisfied with the way I look."

She nodded.

"So what does my crooked nose have to do with your missing husband?" I asked.

She clasped her hands around her legs and pulled them toward her in a classic defensive pose.

"My first husband beat me. One night he went too far even for him, and the next day, when it was clear that my arm was broken, he took me to the nearest walk-in medical center claiming I'd fallen down the cellar stairs. He figured that would be safer than taking me to the hospital. That's how I met Jim. He suspected right away what was going on. He got my husband out of the room on the pretext of filling out some forms and asked me directly if my husband had broken my arm. At first I denied the abuse, as I always had in the past, but Jim persisted. There was just something about him that got me to open up and tell the truth." She smiled. "I'll admit that part of it was physical attraction, but it was combined with a sense of caring and safety I'd never felt from a man before."

"What happened then?"

"The short version of the story is that Jim got me to sneak out of my house and move into a shelter for battered women. He came by frequently as my doctor to check on me, and a relationship naturally developed. When it was time for me to leave the shelter, Jim suggested we go away from the area together and move to Maine. He'd had a job offer here and thought it would be a good chance for me to start over. I divorced my husband, kept my new location a secret, and married Jim."

"I'm sure your ex didn't take that well."

"He would have killed me if he'd ever found out where I was. We lived very cautious lives for the next five years, always wondering if he'd somehow be able to find us. Jim had been very careful not to let anyone know he was involved with me, so they couldn't trace me through him. But even so, we kept an extremely low profile once we got out here. Everything was listed in Jim's name alone, and I never used the Internet."

"What happened after five years?"

"I received word that my ex-husband was killed in a motorcycle accident. I had stayed in touch with one very good and discreet friend from back home. She sent me a letter along with the newspaper clipping. Jim and I went out and had an expensive dinner and drank champagne that night."

I nodded, disappointed. She'd blown away my half-formulated theory that the former husband had finally tracked them down and decided to kill the doctor before moving on to his ex-wife.

"Dr. Jim doesn't sound like the kind of man somebody would want to divorce." I said. "Is he divorcing you, or are you divorcing him?"

Dianne sat back in the sofa, more relaxed now.

"I'm divorcing him. I know, it makes me sound like an ingrate. This young, handsome doctor rides in on his white charger, rescues me from my homicidal husband, and whisks me away to a life of love and safety. And then I go and decide to divorce him."

"So what happened?"

She looked across the room and out the front window at the picture perfect lawn as if trying to recall what had gone wrong.

"I guess you could say that Jim was a rescuer. Once I was no longer in danger, he needed to get back on his horse and find a new damsel in distress to save. Being a doctor, he frequently met women who had some problem or another, and they fell for him as quickly as I had. I know it sounds hard to believe, but you had to know him."

I didn't tell her that I did know him. The fact that I hadn't been particularly attracted to Jim didn't surprise me much. That part of me had been on hold for quite a while. What surprised me more was that he hadn't shown any interest in saving me. I guess I was too challenging a project for him. Even a superman would avoid a kryptonite woman.

"So he started having affairs?" I asked.

"I suppose you could use that word for them. I think of them more as Jim's projects. They were all women who had troubles of one sort or another, and Jim was able to give them comfort. Probably he helped many of them start their lives over again." She paused and gave me a long look. "I want to be fair to him. Jim may have had some of the skills of a gigolo or a con artist, but he wasn't out to get anything for himself."

"What about the sex?"

She gave me a quick nod. "I suppose there was that, but I often wondered whether it repaid all the psychological energy Jim must have had to put into the relationship."

"So he did it all for the thrill of being the knight in shining armor?"

"I've had a long time to think about this," she said with a weak smile that did little to conceal a history of sleepless nights. "Jim's a man who's easily bored. He needs thrills in his life or he becomes depressed. And he gets excitement by being the star of his own story where he saves the helpless woman. It's an addiction that controls his life."

"How did you find out about these 'projects'? Surely, your husband didn't openly share all of this with you."

"No. Jim has never been so insensitive. I trusted him when he told me that he had to go to the hospital at night to visit a patient, and I never checked up on him during the day to see if he took a long lunch. He was also rather careful at first not to be seen with someone else; however, I think he became more casual toward the end. Maybe on some level he had already decided we should conclude our marriage, and this was his indirect way of letting me know. Anyway, it's a small town, and I have a couple of female acquaintances who were more than happy to tell me they had seen my husband having lunch with other women. When I confronted Jim, he admitted everything."

"Did any of these relationships end badly? I imagine some of these women must have been hurt and angry when Jim decided their course of treatment had gone on too long and decided to end it."

"Not that I know of. Jim would have been good at knowing which women would cause trouble, and he'd have avoided them."

Suddenly I knew why I was off his list.

"Also Jim could be very convincing. I can imagine him telling these women that it would be best for them if the relationship ended and getting them to happily go along with it." She gave a short laugh. "I should know. After everything he's done, I still can't say I'm really angry with him."

"What about Lauren Malcolm? Will that relationship last?" The unpleasant thought went through my mind that maybe Lauren had been given her walking papers and done in the doc herself. I wouldn't have figured her for a good liar, but the best ones always come as a surprise.

Dianne smiled sadly. "The poor girl really believes that Jim will marry her once we're divorced."

"You didn't think marriage was going to happen?"

She shook her head. "I'd be surprised if Jim ever married again now that he realizes what a prison it is. No, I think he'd eventually have gotten Lauren to see that a twelve-year age difference is too great, and he'd have her believing she needed to find a younger man who's at the same place in life as she is. He'd convince her that he was the one making a great sacrifice. When she finally left him, she'd feel bad for hurting him and always remember him as her hero."

I must have looked incredulous because Dianne smiled. "You really had to know him. He was very good."

"At manipulating women."

She visibly bridled at my insult to her philandering husband.

"But he always thought he was doing it for the woman's own good," she insisted. "He isn't really a bad person."

In my view, he was the worst.

"I've often felt that in a way the whole thing is my fault," she said.

"How's that?"

"If Jim had never met me, he might not have gotten started on this obsession with rescuing women."

"How do you know you were the first?" I asked.

"Because Jim told me I was."

She stopped suddenly as though hearing her answer for the first time. A hint of worry grew behind her eyes. I figured I'd just given her some food for thought.

"You mentioned to the police that your husband seemed unusually distressed recently. Is that right?"

"I only saw him once last week. He did seem rather quiet and distant. I thought it had something to do with his needing money. He came by because he wanted to withdraw an unusually large amount of money out of our joint savings account, and he needed my permission."

"How much did he need?"

"Ten thousand dollars."

"Why?"

"He said he'd just heard from the caretaker that our summer place up on Sebago Lake needed a new roof."

"And it was going to cost so much?"

Dianne shrugged. "I left that sort of thing up to Jim."

"Could you give the caretaker a call and see if your husband's story holds up?"

"Why would Jim lie?"

"Maybe he needed the money to get away for a while or to give to one of the women he was going to rescue."

"I don't think he'd give our family money to another woman," she said but finally agreed to contact the caretaker.

"To your knowledge, how many women had your husband been involved with in the time since your separation began?"

"It was nine months ago. There are only two I know about. There's Lauren, of course, and for a very brief time, his nurse, Maggie Croyson."

"Was Maggie having problems?"

Dianne hesitated. "I was a little surprised about their involvement myself. She knew Jim so well I thought she'd have realized there was no future with him. But Maggie had just broken up with her longtime boyfriend, so I guess she was vulnerable."

I stood up. "Give me a call when you contact the caretaker."

She said she would and followed me to the door.

"About your nose," she said, as I was about to cross the threshold.

I turned back.

"You really would be quite pretty if you had it fixed."

"I want to be loved for my inner self," I replied.

She nodded and gave me a look that said "fat chance."

CHAPTER 5

It was my day to have lunch with Izzy, my Reiki Master and quasi-therapist, so when I got back to Route 1, I crossed over and headed down the road toward the beach. About halfway along was Larry's Lobster Shack, our usual meeting place. Set up on wooden stilts over the tidal marsh, it was as humble a place as the name suggested, but it had a great deck in back that gave you an unobstructed northern view out over the marsh and inlets. The lobster roll wasn't bad either.

I took my order and went out the back door onto the deck. I knew Izzy would be sitting at a table under the last umbrella checking out the view. He always phoned if he wasn't going to be able to make it. He called himself my healer and said the first responsibility of a good healer is to be reliable so he can provide some stability in the lives of those he's trying to help.

We'd met shortly after I arrived in Cornwall. I was sitting at a table for two in the Blackbird, the only place in Cornwall that deserved to be called a bar. Aside from being a good place to drink, they also had a dance floor and live bands on Friday and Saturday, not that I'd ever been there for the music—way too social for me. I was nursing a club soda and looking around at the small crowd. I wasn't real happy when he came over with a beer in his hand and sat down across from me. Being where I could see other people kept the blues away, but that didn't mean that I wanted to talk to anyone. I liked to imagine I was behind a window made of bulletproof glass where I could watch people but remain completely safe from them. Izzy stepped through my make-believe window as if it wasn't there.

"How long have you been out?" he'd asked me right away.

"Almost two years."

"That long," he said and shook his head.

"How did you know?"

"A young woman with her hair almost whitewalled and a limp is kind of a giveaway."

My hair was pretty much shaved back on the sides but spiky on top.

"I could be a punk rocker who fell off the stage."

He smiled and shook his head again.

"It used to be short all over," I said.

"Why'd you let it grow out on top?" he asked.

"Kind women kept asking me how long I'd been off chemo."

"Why not let it grow out all over?"

"Nostalgia," I replied.

He grinned and sipped his beer.

I studied him for a moment. He was in his late fifties, maybe even his sixties, with a gray ponytail pulled back from a receding hairline. If I'd passed him on the street, I might have thought record producer or civil rights lawyer, but there was a wariness in his eyes that suggested something else.

"Somebody in town probably told you about me," I said, showing him I wasn't easily impressed.

"Could be. But that's beside the point."

"What is the point?" I said impatiently. "If you're trying to pick me up, you're way too old. Anyway, I'm a boatload of trouble."

"I can see that."

He reached across the table and handed me his card. It gave his name and simply said Reiki Master under it. I knew a little about Reiki from my time at the yoga center, but most practitioners there had been ethereal women with fluttering hands and long skirts that swept the floor. I'd never really bought into the healing power of touch or, in the case of some Reiki practitioners, non-touch. Sure it might make you feel better. So would a hot towel. But it sure didn't cure anything.

"So what do you want to do? Wave your hands over my hip? Or do I have to get out of my clothes first?" I added with a smirk.

Izzy shook his head. "The problem isn't in your hip."

"Try walking in my moccasins for a day, and you'd see it differently."

He stared across the room and didn't say anything until I finally broke down.

"Okay, so where is my problem?"

He pointed to my head.

"Cute," I replied.

Before I could say more, he reached across the small table and placed his right hand down hard on the top of my head, like a Bible thumper bringing the power of God. My first reaction was to knock his hand away, but soothing warmth seemed to flow over me, and my hands stayed relaxed on the table. When he finally took his hand away, I blinked, still dazed. Thinking back, I figure he somehow pressed on the cranial nerves and brought on a kind of temporary paralysis. But who knows?

"That was a pretty impressive trick," I said, when my voice started functioning normally again.

"But just a trick," he agreed with a grin. "What you really need is somebody to talk to. Give me a call and we'll set something up."

As he walked away from my table, I figured it would be a cold day in hell before I called him. But the next time the heebie-jeebies came over me, I had called him, and now we met most Mondays. I still didn't know much about him. He insisted that healing was a one-way street: I talked and he listened. I wondered if somewhere in his past he'd earned a string of degrees to put after his name, but we never talked about that either. He'd probably be too embarrassed to admit it even if it were true, like an ex-con talking about his past.

I walked over to the table at Larry's and sat down. Izzy nodded, and we sat for a moment just looking out across the tidal marsh with the ocean on one side and the gentle slope of the sandy cliffs on the other. It was one of those warm days in the very early fall when the summer weather lingers with a nostalgic ripeness. I pushed out from under the umbrella, so I could feel the warmth of the sun on my face and chest. Slowly I could feel the twitching in my mind slow and the pain in my hip ease.

"Too much sun and you'll get cancer," Izzy said without looking at me.

"Cancer won't be what kills me."

"So what have you been up to?" he asked.

I moved back under the umbrella. We both opened our sandwiches and started to eat. My healing sessions with Izzy usually start with the first bite and end when we're through eating. I told him about Lauren, my meeting with Jack, and the visit with Dianne Schianno. He gave a low whistle when I was through.

"That's quite a break from your regular routine, Ali. Usually it's just, I taught yoga, walked on the beach, ate three small meals a day, and tried to sleep."

"That's all it would have been up until today. And I'm already regretting the change."

Izzy grinned.

"And don't tell me this is some kind of breakthrough," I added. "This is a one-time thing, and as soon as it's over, I'm going back to the old solo song and dance."

"Okay."

Izzy's always agreeable. He knows that if he pushes, I'll just come back harder.

We sat there in silence enjoying the quiet of the marsh.

"So why did you agree to help Lauren?" Izzy finally asked. "Was it because of the captain?"

That was the way I always referred to the man who had been my lover in Iraq.

"I suppose he might have had something to do with it. I know being the other woman isn't easy. But that might not be the reason I'm helping her. Who really knows?"

"Yeah. Yeah," Izzy said, waving his hand in the air as if he'd heard me say this before.

And he had. We'd had this conversation over and over. In one of our first chats, he'd asked me why I volunteered for the Army right out of college. He'd wanted to know if it was to spite my liberal, Democratic, the-criminal-is-always-right father, or if it was 9/11, or just a misdirected desire for adventure.

"I don't always agree with my father's politics," I'd answered, "but I sure didn't do it because I agreed with the clueless son of that guy up the road." I'd gestured with my lemonade up the coast toward Kennebunkport.

"So it wasn't politics?" Izzy had asked.

"The American people sent me over there to have my ass blown away. It wasn't the president all by himself. It's living in society that sucks. Once you agree to do that, then you let other people have control over your life."

"So you don't want to be part of society? Are you planning to go live in a cave somewhere?"

"I would if I didn't think they'd still find me. But no, I have to live in society, but I don't have to be part of it. My only loyalty is to myself and to those people I choose to be loyal to."

"That doesn't tell me why you volunteered for the Army," Izzy had persisted.

"I don't give reasons for the things I do because reasons are lies. I don't think any of us can really know why we do what we do. It just happens to us. We wake up one morning and decide to do something, then we make up a story so it sounds as if we're being rational."

Izzy nodded. "So you also don't know why you stopped drinking?"

"I was off it for a while because of the painkillers, then I decided not to do it anymore. And you're right, I don't know why. Maybe someday I'll start drinking again, and I won't know why I did that either. Why does the little ball land on the red rather than the black?"

"So why do you talk to me if reasons don't matter?"

"Because talking to you makes me feel better."

I guess Izzy didn't want to have this discussion again, because after he had waved his hand in the air, he'd slumped back in his chair. We usually argued over something, but I could tell his heart wasn't in it today. He never told me anything about his past, but sometimes when he thought I wasn't looking, I'd catch him with that thousand-yard stare men got who had seen far worse things in combat than I ever had. I wondered whether by healing me he wasn't healing a small part of himself.

"So why are you so down in the dumps?" I finally asked. The worst he could do was not answer.

He shook his head. "I've got another client. She was raped. I'm having a lot of trouble getting her to trust me."

I nodded. "You're a man. You're the enemy."

He sighed. "Is that the way it is for you? Two opposing teams?"

"I don't have a team. Life is an individual sport."

He gave me a shrewd look. "Were you ever raped?"

I was tempted to get up and leave. But I wasn't finished with my lobster roll.

"Almost."

"Tell me about it."

"Almost doesn't count."

"Why don't you tell me about it anyway? Maybe it will help me with my other client."

"I doubt it will help."

"You never know."

I cleared my throat. "I had a first sergeant in Iraq. He was in his forties and sort of old school. Probably didn't have much education and had worked his way up through the ranks by being tough and savvy. A lot of the younger, more educated NCOs, didn't care much for him because he didn't bother trying to win people over, but I always got along all right with him."

"You were a sergeant then."

"Yeah. I was a staff sergeant, so we worked together a lot. He would give me some advice once in a while. Sometimes it was technical stuff about how to handle evidence or subdue troublemakers. Other times it was career stuff about how to get along in the Army."

"What happened?"

"Once night I was all alone in the female NCO quarters. There were two other women who lived there, but they both had night duty. I was surprised to see him come in the women's barracks, because it was pretty much off limits to men. Before I knew it he was on top of me, trying to tear my clothes off. I pushed him away and he punched me in the side of the head. Fortunately I stayed conscious and managed to get enough distance from him that I could head-butt him in the nose. That backed him up enough that I could roll off my bunk. He stood there with blood dripping from his nose like a bear that'd been stung by a bee. His expression said he couldn't believe I'd done that."

"I don't imagine he was happy."

"He told me that he was going to give me duties that would make my life such a living hell, I'd be back begging for him to do anything he wanted to me. I believed him. I'd seen him do the same thing to break guys he'd taken a dislike to."

"Did you go to your superior officer?" Izzy asked.

I shook my head.

"Surely in this day and age, they'd take a charge of attempted rape seriously."

"Maybe. Although you have to remember it would have been a case of M.P.s investigating an M.P. first sergeant. You never know how it might turn out. But even if by luck it did go my way, I knew what would happen. The worst they'd do to him was to force him to retire—he already had his twenty years in. But the world of military police is pretty small, and I knew the case would follow me to wherever I was posted. I'd always be the woman who accused her first sergeant of rape. People would wonder who was telling the truth, and none of the men I worked with would trust me again. My career would pretty much be over."

"So what did you do?"

"I handled it my own way."

"Which was how?"

"Are you sure you want to know about this? It isn't going to help this other woman."

"It might."

I shrugged. "The next night I left my bunk around midnight and looked for a nice dark spot between the male NCO quarters and the latrine. It had to be a place where I wouldn't be easily seen, but close enough that I could identify who was coming along."

"Weren't there any lights?"

"Yeah. A couple of floodlights. I took the blanket from my bunk to put over me, so I'd blend in with the shadows. Just like most of the other NCOs, the first sergeant liked his beer, so I was pretty certain he'd wander along some time. I watched for the next three nights, until I knew his pattern of getting up. The next day I swiped a blanket out of supply and slipped into the mess hall to borrow the long-handled wrench they used to work on the sink when it got clogged."

"You didn't think they would miss it?" Izzy asked.

"If the drain backed up, I guess they might have. That was the one part of my plan I had to leave to luck. You can't control everything."

He nodded.

"Anyway, that night I waited. The first sergeant went past me. I figured I'd hold off until he returned because there was a light in the latrine, so he'd have lost some of his night vision. When he came out and went past me, I rushed up and tapped him on the back of the head with the wrench. Not too hard, just enough to daze him but leave him standing. I threw the blanket over his head, so he wouldn't recognize me and to help smother any sounds. Then I moved around to the front and hit him on the side of his right knee with the wrench. I used a full baseball swing and really put some muscle into it. I could hear the knee pop."

I paused and took a sip of my lemonade.

"Did he make a lot of noise?"

"More than I thought he would, given the blanket. I debated doing his left knee as well, but decided that was probably overkill. Plus I was afraid that someone might have heard him. So I left the blanket over his head, disappeared into the dark-ness, and in five minutes I was back in my own bunk."

"What happened to the first sergeant?"

"They evacuated him out the next morning. I guess his knee was pretty messed up."

"There must have been an investigation."

"Sure. But the guys conducting it mostly hated him anyway, so nobody tried too hard. I think everyone was afraid if they were really thorough, they'd just end up getting a friend in trouble."

Izzy was quiet for a long moment, then he said, "I wonder why he suddenly tried to rape you."

"I heard later that he'd gotten a 'Dear John' letter from his wife. I guess it sent him around the bend. She hurt him, so he was going to hurt me. Nobody likes to be a victim."

"Too bad it had to play out that way," Izzy said.

"Yeah, he was like a father to me."

Izzy gave me a long look. "You were wrong, though."

"About what?"

"I think this *is* going to help my other client."

I smiled. "Yeah, I know where she can get a wrench."

CHAPTER 6

After leaving Izzy, I spent a good chunk of the afternoon walking on the beach. I don't teach on Monday nights, so I figured this would be a good way to get well and truly tired. I've found that when I'm exhausted, my mind starts to focus on the present and stops jumping all around like a monkey in the trees, as the Buddhists say. By the time I'd finished supper, however, I still couldn't get my mind to stay focused on the magazine open on my lap or the television playing across the room. I kept picturing Dr. Jim on that day when he'd taken the shrapnel out of my hip. As much as I had resisted his wife's upbeat opinion of him, I had to admit he might be the kind of guy who tried to help people in his own messed-up way. Maybe he was manipulative with women, but he had taken some of my pain away that day. That put him in a pretty select group of men.

Originally I'd planned to call Lauren a little later on and tell her what I'd learned. I figured a call would pretty much end my obligation to her. If Jack found out any more, he'd pass it on to me and I would tell her, although I had a feeling this was going to be one of the world's many unsolved missing persons cases. Since Dr. Jim wasn't a child, there'd be no pictures on milk cartons or tearful parents on television pleading for information on the whereabouts of their loved one, and eventually folks would write his disappearance off as either a possible suicide or a case of a guy who decided to start his life over again, severing all ties to the past.

Like I said, blowing off Lauren was what I had planned to do, but now I felt maybe I owned Dr. Jim a little more. So at around seven o'clock, the same time Dr. Jim had left his apartment last Thursday, I left mine and headed out to Turtle Island. It was a nice night, so I figured I wasn't making much of a sacrifice. The worst that would happen was that I'd come back as ignorant as when I left, but with a few extra lungfuls of sea air, more tired and ready to sleep.

By the time I turned off Route 1 and went over the short causeway, long shadows were starting to fall. Turtle Island had an abandoned feeling, as though everyone but me had gotten word of an emergency evacuation. The neighborhood of older houses was quiet in the special sad, nostalgic way that bustling areas feel after everyone has left. There was still enough light to read the street signs if I squinted, and there were not many streets to choose from. So I easily found my way to the end of Monroe where it dead-ended into the sand. I parked close to where I figured Dr. Jim had ended his last known drive.

I walked down the street and out onto the loose sand. It slid away treacherously beneath my feet, putting an extra strain on my bad hip. The darkness erased the defining edges of my perception like a few shots of a single malt scotch used to do for me in an earlier time, and things began to blur into one another. I worked my way through the deep sand like a geriatric camel until I reached the firmer packed stuff by the water's edge. I carefully stayed out of reach of the surf, and turned my back on the ocean, hoping it wouldn't be insulted and send a sneaky wave washing over my athletic shoes.

I studied the houses within view of the beach. If any house had lights on, someone might be living there who had seen the doc arrive last week. I figured the police had already canvassed the neighborhood, but you never know if they might have been unlucky enough to knock on the door when a witness didn't happen to be home. If so, my luck wasn't running much better. I saw nothing but the looming shadows of houses, and no sign of human habitation.

I stood there for several minutes enjoying the feel of the breeze. I looked up and down the beach and back out at the ocean. I tried to put myself in Dr. Jim's frame of mind. Maybe it had been a more moonlit night last Thursday, but on this cloudy evening the ocean seemed like a restless, menacing thing, not a friend that would invite a person to a peaceful, serene death. I wondered what could have frightened the doctor into taking this way out, if that was actually what had happened.

I made my way back toward the street. As I passed a large bush that, against all odds, seemed to be thriving on the edge of the sand, I heard a rustling sound. I spun to my left. I could see a shadowy form hiding there and charged forward. I've always found that your odds are better if you attack first.

"Mister, mister, don't hurt me, mister. I'm an old man," a reedy voice said. He stood up and put his arms in the air as though this was a Western-style hold-up.

"I'm not a mister," I said, advancing closer to him. Since I was wearing my usual uniform of jeans, a denim shirt, and a zip jacket, I could understand how it might have been hard to tell in the deep twilight. I took out a pocket flashlight and shined it on him. He was thin. His shirt was out of his pants and only partially buttoned, and his hair stood on end like tufts of cotton. He could have been an escapee from somewhere, but the three-pronged cane he clutched in his right hand suggested it hadn't been a real speedy getaway. A loose-lipped smile came over his face.

"Are you going to take your clothes off, too, like the other one?"

"Don't hold your breath," I snapped, wondering what erotic fantasy I'd stepped into. Then I paused and gave his comment some thought. "What 'other one'?"

"Take that light out of my face and maybe I'll tell you," he said slyly.

I lowered the beam.

"She came walking up from the beach, same way you just did. She walked over to a car that was parked right near that streetlight."

The nearest streetlight was in a strange spot, about fifty feet beyond the last house and before you reached my car. Maybe it was put in so people could see after dark as they walked back from the beach.

"She was wearing one of those outfits that the kids on the surfboards wear. You know, the kinda thing that makes you look like a frogman."

"A wetsuit."

"Yeah, that's it. And she was carrying a short surfboard of some kind, too. She walked right past me just like you did, but I guess her ears weren't as good as yours. She never knew I was here."

"What did she do?"

"Walked right over to her car and opened the trunk."

"Do you know what kind of car it was?"

"Nah. All I recognize are the old Fords and Chevys. This wasn't one of them."

"Okay. What happened next?"

"She shoved her board inside. Then she just stood there and bold as could be took her suit off. Right out in the open. Naked as a jaybird, she was."

I glanced around the neighborhood again, still no light on in any of the windows. Her car would have been slightly down the slope, hard to see even if someone was at home and looking.

"Then she went around to the back door, took some clothes out, and got dressed."

"What did she look like?"

"She was naked."

"Yeah, I got that part. I was hoping for a more detailed description."

He gave a rheumy cough. "I'd say she was around average height for a woman. I can't see real well in the dark, but I'd say not as tall as you." He paused. "To tell you the truth my eyes aren't all that good, and she was kind of far away. I would have tried to get closer, but I was afraid I might scare her off."

"Are you sure she was naked?"

I heard him chuckle. "I'm not blind. That part I'm sure about."

"So I guess you wouldn't have any idea of hair color or whether she was fat or thin."

"Her hair was dark. She was no blonde, that much I know. I'd guess she wasn't real fat or real thin—more in between. Say, I'm getting kind of cold out here. Maybe if you got any more questions you should give me a few dollars for my time and discomfort."

"Maybe I should have the police run you in as a peeping tom."

He straightened up as much as he could. "I wasn't peeping. I was standing in a public place. She was flaunting herself."

The outrage in his voice made me smile—a rare enough occurrence that I reached in my pocket and got out my wallet. I took out a ten. Shining the light on it so he could see, I handed it over. He took it in a bony, shaking hand.

"Hey, thanks a lot."

"What's your name?" I asked.

"Harry Link. What's yours?"

I told him my name.

"What night did you see all of this?" I asked.

"Jeez, the days all kind of blur together when you stop working. I know it was last week some time, because the woman from the church came to visit me on Sunday, and it was before that."

"Was there another car parked along the road down here?"

"Now that you say it, I think there was. It was further down, where that one is now," he said, gesturing toward mine.

This told me he'd seen this woman on Thursday night when Dr. Jim went missing. By Friday night, his car had already been found and towed away by the police.

"Did you see the driver of the other car?"

"Nope. Both cars were already here when I walked down the road."

"What time was that?"

"Well, I usually come along like I did tonight, around eight. But that night I was watching something on television and didn't get out till closer to eight-thirty or even a little later."

"Why do you remember that?" One of the things I'd learned as an M.P. was to be suspicious of people who suddenly get precise. It's often a sign they're making things up to please you.

He cleared his throat loudly. "I figured maybe I'd get to see her put on a show again if I came down around the same time the next night. So I checked the time and made a point of waiting until eight-thirty on Friday to take my walk."

"Any luck?"

"Nah. Just as well," he said with a chuckle, "it might have been too much for my heart."

"Do you live on the island?"

"Sure do. I live in a small cape way back almost to the bridge—had it for a dog's age. The place was our summer home. We'd come out here with the kids every summer. After I retired, my wife and me figured to live here year round. She's been dead a while now. I suppose I should live in closer to things, but it seems like too much trouble to move."

"What about your kids?"

"They live near Boston. Every once in a while one of them comes out and says my 'quality of life' is lousy, whatever that is. But I guess as long as I can walk around and drive enough to get to the store and buy groceries, I'll be all right."

"Didn't the police ask you about a car parked down here? They went door-to-door through the neighborhood."

"I sleep a lot during the day, and I'm a real sound sleeper. Even when I'm awake, I don't always bother to answer the door. The police aren't going to come around asking me about that woman, are they?" he asked in a suddenly worried voice. "Nothing happened to her, did it? I know from television how they're always arresting some guy over a sex thing. I'm no pervert."

"Nothing's happened to her as far as I know. And you won't get into trouble if you talk to them."

"All right," he said doubtfully. "Well, I think I'll walk back home now. I really am getting kinda cold."

"Do you want to ride back with me?" I asked, not really crazy about the idea.

"Nah. Thanks anyway. I don't want to get home too soon. It'll just make the night seem longer. It's long enough as it is when you're alone."

I knew what he meant, but kept quiet. I didn't want this to turn into a pity party. We said our good-byes and went our separate ways. As I drove past him slowly making his way up the street, I gave a gentle toot on my horn.

I spent the rest of the short drive home wondering who the naked woman was on the beach that night, and whether she had anything to do with the missing Dr. Jim.

CHAPTER 7

I slept well. That doesn't sound like a lot to most people. But to those of us who plan our days so we can get to sleep at night, it's a real accomplishment. The problem is that once you achieve it, you have to start all over the next day. I went out on my balcony and did the advanced Sun Salutation for fifteen minutes. This is the sequence that includes the Virabhadrasana, the Warrior I posture, which always gives me power for the day.

Finally I knelt and lowered myself back into a sitting position between my legs. It's called the Hero pose. At the yoga center I was told that this was a great way to keep your hip from freezing up after an injury. I hoped they were right about its doing some good, because the pain as the scarred muscles slowly stretched was excruciating. I gritted my teeth and stayed in the posture for a full two minutes. My hip would never be normal, but I hoped that, if I kept stretching, it wouldn't get worse and might actually show some improvement.

Slowly getting to my feet, I leaned on the railing of my balcony and looked across the tidal marsh. Today was another clear, crisp early fall day when everything seems brighter than real life, as if the world had been washed in one of those detergents that promise extra brightening.

Although I have this great view from my condo, the scenery wasn't why I had purchased it. When I first moved to Cornwall, one of the things that worried me was that by living in a small town I'd have neighbors who would want to get to know me and then try to draw me into becoming part of the local community. To avoid this would have required rudeness and led to my developing a reputation as an eccentric, which would have defeated my ultimate intention of keeping a low profile. I got around this by buying into a condominium complex where the folks who owned the units rented them out to weekly vacationers and rarely came to stay there themselves. This worked well for me. The condo came completely furnished, so I didn't have to make a lot of decisions. And I kind of liked trying to figure out what the previous owners had been like, based on their taste in home decor. I also enjoyed the occasional surprise of finding something unusual in the back of a drawer.

More importantly, during the summer the complex had been filled with transients who assumed I was one of them and paid no attention to me. I couldn't have been more anonymous in the midst of a crowd if I'd lived in Manhattan. The weeks since Labor Day had seen a steep decline in the number of cars in the parking lot during the week, although the place still filled up on the weekends. I suspected this wouldn't last much past Columbus Day, and soon I would be one of a very select handful continuing to occupy one of the sixty units. I was looking forward to a quiet and uncomplicated winter, highlighted by solitary walks on empty beaches.

My desire to avoid entanglements was also why I had opened my own business. If you work for others, they feel entitled to ask personal questions with the expectation of answers. When you're the employer, your employees usually don't feel they have the right to interrogate you. Of course, I didn't really need to work at all. My grandmother on my mother's side had a fair amount of money she'd inherited from her own family, and she'd set up a trust fund for my brothers and me that gave us each a sizeable chunk of cash on our twenty-first birthday. I think she had always felt guilty that Mom had disappeared and left us, although ultimately I think she blamed my father for driving her away. Grandma's will had been set up to clearly and unbreakably keep this money out of the hands of my father. I suspect my grandmother knew that if he had access to it, the money would have gone to fund a retirement home for elderly serial killers or something else equally dear to Dad's lawyerly heart.

At any rate, Grandma had given me the luxury of financial independence as long as I invested prudently and remained reasonably frugal. Why do I work, then? Because of the one thing money can't give you—structure. I needed a place to go every morning, even if I had little to do there except sit behind my desk and try to master the computer. Without structure, I knew that eventually I'd be unable to get out of bed in the morning.

After finishing my daily yoga practice, I showered and had cereal, toast, juice, and coffee. I don't know if breakfast is nutritionally the most important meal of the day like the experts claim, but for me it's the first step in a psychically healthy day. Mentally I can check off the first of the three meals that a normal person eats. The closer I come to normality in the little things, the more I can aspire to normality in the big things.

I called the police station to tell Jack about my conversation with Mr. Link, but he wasn't in, so I left a message for him to call me. Then I headed down to the yoga shop, as I like to think of it. When I got there, I began by pulling the battered tin cash box out of the lower right drawer of the desk where I ask the teachers to stash it if I'm not around when they're done for the evening. Since both Julie and Karen had taught last night, there was more bookkeeping than usual to do. In my short time running the business I'd discovered that the people who take yoga don't intentionally deadbeat you when it comes to paying, but their memories seem to have large gaps. By holding them to account, I feel I'm doing a service by helping them remain in touch with the world.

When I finished, I walked out into the lobby. There's a long mirror at one end. It's right next to a folding screen for the occasions when someone wants to change into or out of street clothes. I stood in front of the mirror and closed my right eye and let my left eye study my face, then I closed my left eye and let my right do the same. Each side of my face was clear to me when I looked through one eye. However, when I opened both eyes, my crooked nose seemed to dominate the landscape, forcing my other features into a blurry background, as though I were taking portrait pictures with the camera setting on landscape. I was doing the opening and closing thing for around the third time, when the door opened behind me. I spun around, wrenching my hip and staggering slightly.

Karen walked into the room. A tentative smile formed on her lips, as if she wanted to ask what I had been doing but was afraid it might be too personal a question. Some women could have said they were checking their makeup, but my face was too obviously unadorned.

"I've been thinking about getting my nose straightened," I blurted out.

Karen nodded and came closer. She stared up at my face for several seconds while I stood there, rigid, like a hunting dog pointing at a covey of grouse. If I'd thought that Karen's maternal attitude extended to the polite lie, I was wrong.

"Well, it would definitely improve your looks," she said. "How did you break it?"

"A childhood accident," I lied.

"Do you want to be better looking?"

I stared at her for a long moment, carefully considering my answer to that good but unusual question. Karen must have thought I was somehow offended, because she blushed.

"I know most people would want to, but you've always struck me as someone who's above that sort of thing."

My continued silence seemed to unnerve her still further.

"I mean, being a yoga teacher and all, I thought that maybe being healthy was more important to you than appearance."

"Those are all good points," I admitted finally. "I'll have to give them further thought."

Karen smiled and visibly relaxed, as if she had just passed a difficult exam.

I glanced over at my Buddha clock.

"Aren't you a little early for class? It's only eight-thirty."

She nodded. "I wanted to talk to you about Lauren Malcolm."

Karen sat down on the changing bench along the one wall. That left me looking down on her from above, so she had to crane her neck up at what was no doubt a painful angle to look at me. I decided that as little as I wanted to talk about Lauren, I shouldn't take it out on Karen, so I sat on the bench across from her, stretching out my leg to relieve the pressure on my hip.

"Lauren told me about Dr. Jim," Karen began. "She also said that she had asked you to help her."

I nodded.

"I'm not sure that's a good thing."

"Neither am I," I replied.

That seemed to surprise Karen, and she paused before going on.

"Lauren and I went out for coffee after class yesterday for some girl talk, you know."

I nodded, pretending that meant something to me.

"She's been in a number of bad relationships, and all of them were the kind where the man was somehow unattainable, either married or seriously involved with someone else."

"I see," I said, wondering when she was going to get to the point.

Karen's face turned sad. "It really is a shame when a nice, good-looking girl like that doesn't have enough self-respect. It makes you wonder what her family was like."

"Is that the problem, a lack of self-respect?" I asked.

"Certainly. Lauren doesn't think she's good enough to be anything other than a man's little piece of fluff on the side. If she considered herself good enough to be a man's wife, she wouldn't always be getting involved with attached men. She has a poor self-image," Karen explained with a patient expression, as if I shouldn't have needed all of this to be spelled out.

I wondered if a solution to Lauren's problem would be to start dating single men whose lack of self-respect exceeded her own. I didn't think Karen would appreciate my suggestion. I also didn't think she would care to hear my opinion that this might not have anything to do with any deep psychological problems; maybe Lauren just happened to meet a lot of interesting men who were married and not too fussy about their vows. Sometimes beneath the surface, there's just more surface.

"So what does this have to do with my helping her find Dr. Jim?" I asked.

"I don't think she needs him back in her life," Karen declared. Her face took on a look of common-sense firmness.

"Won't she just find another married man as a replacement? Maybe one who treats her worse than Dr. Jim did," I said.

"We have to break her cycle of addiction before we can effect a cure."

I blinked and waited for an explanation.

"Of course, there will be a period of mourning for her lost relationship. But if we can get her into therapy during that time, before she finds a replacement, then we might be able to turn her life around."

"Sort of like intervening between an alcoholic's first and second drink?" I asked.

Karen stared at me, trying to decide if I was being flippant. Since I needed her as a teacher, I decided to build a bridge rather than a wall, to use an expression that she would doubtlessly appreciate.

"Like an alcoholic, doesn't she have to want to change?" I asked.

Karen nodded. "She does want to change. That's why she came to you for help."

"She wanted my help getting Dr. Jim back."

"It only appeared that way. On a deeper level, she was looking to you to tell her she should forget about him and take a new direction in life. Lauren admires you, and hearing you say she should move on would validate that course of action for her."

"So I should tell her what exactly?"

"That it's very unlikely anyone will ever know what happened to Dr. Jim, and she should get on with her life. Then open up the possibility to Lauren of getting professional treatment. I'll guide her in that direction as well. Between us, we should be able to rescue her."

I nodded. "Eventually I may tell her just that—at least the part about Dr. Jim not reappearing."

"Why not tell her now?" Karen asked with a patient smile.

"Because I don't know if it's true. Imagine what it would do to my credibility with Lauren if I said Dr. Jim is gone forever, then he pops up next week with a big smile on his face and a story about having to rush off to a medical conference in Las Vegas."

It was Karen's turn to pause and think things over.

"That's a good point. How long do you think it will take, assuming Dr. Jim doesn't show up, until you'd feel comfortable telling her there's no point pursuing the matter further?"

"A couple more days," I replied off the top of my head, anxious to end this conversation.

"That should be fine. Maybe we can talk about it more then."

I stared at her until she glanced at the clock.

"Oh, look at the time. I'd better go over my plans for class," Karen said, getting to her feet and walking toward me. She reached out and touched my shoulder. "I'm glad we had this conversation."

I nodded. That made one of us.

I got to my feet and almost took a last glance over my shoulder into the mirror. But I knew I'd seen enough of myself for one day. "I'm perfect the way I am," some folks would repeat over and over during yogic training. I always doubted whether such exaggeration was of real benefit. I certainly wasn't perfect the way I was. But at least I was familiar with my current self. Even a change that might seem to be for the better could have consequences, like the ripples of a small rock thrown into a pond that eventually disrupted everything else. I couldn't take the chance. My nose would stay the way it was.

The door opened again before I could make it back to my office, and Jack walked into the lobby.

"Hello, Alison."

I've talked to Jack a number of times after class, but it suddenly struck me that he always called me Alison, never Ali. Ali was an abbreviation my father hung on me because, as he often said in a disappointed tone, it captured my nature as a tomboy. I'd managed to partially escape it in the Army where I was often referred to as Randall, last names being more the norm. I had avoided it altogether in Iraq, a country where "Ali" seemed to be part of the name of most local males. But when the captain and I were alone, he used it as a term of intimacy and endearment, and I didn't disabuse him. And although I'd come to use the nickname myself, I liked the fact that Jack didn't. It was nice to know someone thought of me as somewhat feminine.

"Hello, Jack," I finally replied.

The long delay between his greeting and my response didn't seem to bother him. My conversational delays as I try to put things together make lots of people nervous, but Jack had spent the time looking around the lobby as if his "hello" had been a challenging question requiring adequate time to formulate an answer.

"You left a message saying you wanted to talk to me," he said.

"That's right." I heard the thumping on the steps of the first arrivals for Karen's class and gestured that we should go into my office.

Once inside I closed the door, knowing we would need privacy. My office had always seemed easily large enough for two before, but once we were seated, it suddenly felt crowded. And it wasn't because Jack's slender six-foot frame was sprawling across the room. In fact, he had made himself rather compact and sat with his legs crossed as if he knew I had little tolerance for invasion of my space. I controlled the claustrophobic tightness in my chest, and proceeded to give Jack a summary of my conversation with Mr. Link.

When I was through he nodded. "Now that we have a name it won't be any problem getting his address. I'll send someone around to talk to him, although I doubt we'll learn any more than you did. I wonder who the woman was. Do you think she had anything to do with Dr. Jim?"

"A lot of women seem to have been involved with the doctor," I said. I told Jack what I had learned from Mrs. Schianno.

He shook his head. "As I told you before, I'd heard a few rumors that Schianno might have taken his bedside manner a bit too far, but there were never any complaints from his patients, so it didn't become a police matter."

"And according to his wife, these affairs ended amicably."

"It might have been amicable from the woman's point of view, but if their husbands got wind of an affair with the doctor, things could have turned ugly," Jack said. "That could be what happened. Maybe Dr. Jim practiced his particular brand of sexual healing on the wrong man's wife."

"As far as I can tell, Dr. Jim hasn't been involved with anyone other than Lauren for the past eight months. Right before that he had a brief affair with Maggie Croyson, his nurse. She's single, and according to Mrs. Schianno, she'd already broken off with her boyfriend before her involvement with the doctor. So there doesn't seem to be any outraged husband or boyfriend in the picture. Of course, I suppose it's possible that the husband of a woman from the doc's past might have just learned about the affair and sought revenge."

"I wonder if Maggie would be able to give us a list of the names of the patients with whom Dr. Jim was involved. She also could tell us if there were any angry husbands coming around looking to pin the doc's ears back," Jack said.

I nodded. "That sounds like a good line of inquiry."

Jack gave me a smile. "Why don't you follow up on it, then?"

I frowned.

"Or maybe you'd like to come with me to the Donut Hole for a cup of coffee and a chocolate dipped. While we're there, I can use my masculine charms to convince you to help me."

"Don't you have any officers who can question Maggie?" I asked.

"This is the sort of thing better handled by a female officer, and the only woman on the force is currently away at the state police academy for further training."

"Maybe you could use those masculine charms on Maggie," I suggested.

He shook his head sadly. "I can't just turn them on and off like that. I have to really be motivated."

"Well, in order to avoid the danger of being exposed to your charms and a high-fat pastry, I'll agree right here and now to help you with Maggie."

I thought an expression of disappointment flashed across his face.

"I appreciate that, Alison," he said, slowly getting to his feet. "Maybe we can have a donut another time."

"And I have to say I do admire you, Jack."

"Why is that?" he asked suspiciously.

"Not many police officers would have the self-confidence to admit they like donuts."

He looked at me in surprise. "Why I do believe that you have a sense of humor underneath the serious exterior, Ms. Randall."

I shook my head. "The donut thing was just an observation."

CHAPTER 8

I closed the door to my office right after Jack left so I wouldn't have to make small talk with the people coming to take Karen's class. I called the number of Dr. Jim's practice and got through to Maggie. When I told her the police had asked me to speak to her, she said she had already spoken with the police and had nothing more to tell about the doctor's disappearance. But after I made up a soothing story about how this was all part of our need to bring the entire team up to speed, she reluctantly agreed to see me. Since the doctor covering for Dr. Jim was only able to come in during the afternoons, there were no patients scheduled for the morning, so we decided I should stop by right away. When I heard *"Om"* chanted three times and knew that Karen had officially begun her class, I slipped out of my office and down the stairs.

The clinic where Dr. Jim plied his trade was only two miles to the northwest, so I was there in ten minutes. A modern one-story building set back from the road with lots of grass and well-maintained landscaping around it, the clinic was the place to go in Cornwall if you had any kind of medical emergency, because they would see you without an appointment. There were doctors in the surrounding towns, and you could always go down to York if you needed the hospital emergency room, but most people in Cornwall found themselves at the clinic for the sudden injuries and unexpected accidents that life seems to dole out to everyone.

The sign at the entrance listed Maggie as a physician's assistant. Dianne Schianno and Lauren had both referred to her as a nurse. I wondered if they had intentionally demoted her out of jealousy over her romantic relationship with the doctor.

Once in the waiting room I went up to the sliding glass window. A slender young woman wearing glasses that had been trendy in the fifties and were now in style again, pushed one side open.

"I'm sorry, but the doctor isn't here right now," she told me. There was a quiver to her lips that suggested the absence of Dr. Jim upset her on more than a professional level.

"I'm here to see Maggie Croyson."

"Do you have an appointment?"

"I talked to her ten minutes ago on the phone, and she told me to come right over."

"Have you been here before for treatment?"

"This isn't a medical visit."

She gave me a puzzled look.

"Maybe you could just tell Maggie that Ali Randall is here," I suggested.

She gave me a suspicious look, then carefully closed the sliding glass window and got on the phone. I wondered whether she was calling Maggie or the police. The answer came a few seconds later. A petite woman wearing a nicely tailored blouse and stylish slacks opened the door to the waiting room. She was in her early thirties with a great haircut and a perky attitude. She was everything I'm not. She didn't seem to recognize me from when I'd been in several months ago to be treated, which I figured was just as well.

"Alison, you can come right this way," she said with an inviting smile, as if I were her favorite patient.

I followed her down the hall, trying not to favor my bad hip too much. Doctors' offices always make me more gimpy than usual. She opened the third door on the right and I stepped inside. It was an examination room. I paused for a moment, wondering if Maggie was confused about the reason for my visit. I looked around for a place to sit. Maggie had already taken the stool on wheels that the doctor usually tooled around on, so I hopped up on the examining table.

"Since I'm the one who was supposed to be asking the questions, I think our positions should be reversed," I said.

"Sorry, force of habit," she said, but did not offer to switch places. "I can't take you into one of the offices, because they're only supposed to be used by the doctors."

"No problem."

"Like I said on the phone, I'm not sure what more I can tell you about Dr. Schianno. I have no idea where he went."

"I gather from what I've heard from Mrs. Schianno that Dr. Jim sometimes developed a personal relationship with some of his female patients."

Some of the perkiness left her face. "She told you that?"

I nodded. "I was wondering if you could give me a list of those patients."

"Oh, I wouldn't be able to tell you anything about that."

"But you do know he cheated on his wife?"

I could see she was about to deny it, then she paused.

"My sister is a waitress at Ramondi's, a restaurant just outside of Portland. She told me she saw Dr. Jim there a couple of times with different women. But I don't know whether they were patients or not."

"You knew about the doctor and Lauren Malcolm. She was a patient."

"But that was after the doctor and his wife separated."

"So was the relationship between you and the doctor," I said.

Her mouth opened and closed several times like a fish struggling for air.

"Did Dianne Schianno tell you that?" she asked.

I nodded.

"Oh, God. How did she find out?"

"She didn't say. Maybe the doctor himself told her. Or maybe you made the mistake of going out to lunch with him. Your sister's probably not the only one who tells tales."

I watched her think back, and a worried look came over her face.

"I wouldn't let it bother me," I said. "I doubt that Mrs. Schianno cares much at this point."

"It was only a short fling right after I broke up with my boyfriend. Jim was just trying to help me get over the worst of it. He was good that way."

"So I've heard. Then he met Lauren and decided she was the one he wanted to play house with for the long run."

Her lips twisted into a scornful smile. "I doubt that very much."

"Lauren thought so."

"I know. I've heard from her a few times since Jim disappeared."

"But you don't think their relationship was actually going to work out that way."

Maggie put her hand on the examining table and leaned forward so her face was close to my bad hip. I was wondering if she planned to kiss it and make it all better. If that worked, it would be worth an article in a medical journal.

"Look, Jim was a lot of wonderful things. He was a great doctor. He had a natural way with people that put them at ease, and he knew how to listen. How many doctors—how many men— know how to do that? I can't put it into words, but there was something a little magical about him."

"Was there a downside to all this abracadabra?" I asked.

Maggie nodded. "He had to keep moving on."

"So he cast his spell, then went on to the next woman."

She frowned. "That makes him sound like he was just another guy who's good at conning women into bed, then gets bored and hits the road."

"It does have that sound to it," I admitted.

"The difference was that you knew he really cared about you. And you really did feel better about yourself afterwards. There was none of the self-loathing you usually have after someone dumps you." She paused for a moment, as if remembering something from her past. "It's like thinking back on a perfect spring day. You're sorry it's passed, but you're glad that you had the chance to experience it."

I gave her a flat stare.

"Haven't you ever felt that way about someone?" she asked.

"I've usually thought the guy who dumped me deserved to die," I said. "But maybe that's just me."

"And you never knew Jim."

I let that pass. "But Lauren wasn't at the fond farewell stage. Could she have gotten angry if Dr. Jim cut her loose?"

Maggie shook her head. "He'd have let her down so easy, she wouldn't have felt the bump."

"I don't know. She seems kind of fragile to me."

"I'm sure lots of them were. Jim was attracted to women in need."

"But you don't know any names?"

She shook her head stubbornly. I didn't believe her. She would have watched how Dr. Jim's female patients acted around him and known.

"How about angry husbands? They might see Dr. Jim's healing methods as a bit unorthodox."

I could see by her eyes that something had occurred to her.

"There was one guy who came by the office on a day when Jim wasn't here and made a scene. He kept shouting that Jim was messing with the wrong man, and that he'd kill him if he didn't leave his wife alone. It was pretty scary. Fortunately the only patient here was an elderly woman who was deaf."

"Who was the guy?"

She hesitated.

"You probably should have reported this when it happened. I can get a detective over here with one phone call if you'd rather tell him."

"His name is Jed Turlow."

"So what happened between him and Dr. Jim?"

"Turlow was a wife beater. Jim convinced Turlow's wife to leave him, and set her up in a shelter." Maggie sat back and made a wringing motion with her hands. "When Jim told me about her, I got worried. I worried that the next time this guy came in, he might have a gun and shoot up the place."

"Did you let Jim know you felt that way?"

She nodded. "He told me he'd take care of it."

"Did he?"

"A few days later, he said he'd talked to Turlow. He explained to him that his wife would press charges against him if he didn't leave us alone. Jim warned him that the medical evidence conclusively proved abuse, and he got the impression Turlow was frightened enough to let the whole thing drop. He already had a new girlfriend anyway."

"Can you tell me anything else about this guy?"

"Aside from the fact that he was scary, I've heard he owns a lumberyard out near North Berwick."

"When did all this take place?"

"A little over a month ago."

"And you haven't seen Turlow since then?"

She shook her head.

"Was Dr. Jim romantically involved with Mrs. Turlow?"

"I don't think so. Jim said he picked her up at home when

her husband was at work and took her to the shelter. She only stayed there for a couple of nights and then moved out of the state."

"Okay, other than Turlow, you can't give me the names of any other women who were the recipients of Dr. Jim's special healing powers," I said, trying hard to keep any sarcasm out of my voice.

"No. Jim never talked about it. I would just be guessing based on the way some of his women patients acted, and it wouldn't be right for me to do that. Plus, I really don't think he's been doing much of that sort of thing since Dianne threw him out. Her decision to end their marriage really shook him up."

"Did Dr. Jim seem to be more worried or upset than usual during the week or so before he disappeared?"

"Now that you mention it, he did seem to have something on his mind. He was distracted. On several occasions I had to repeat things I said to him about a patient's treatment. That was unusual. When it came to work Jim was very focused. And he was more abrupt than I've ever known him to be. Not rude exactly, but more like he didn't have the time to pay attention to what was going on around him."

"Do you know what was wrong?"

She shook her head. "I asked him about it, and he just said it was a small personal problem, and he was planning to resolve it soon."

I slid off the examining table, and Maggie stood. It was the easiest examination I'd ever had.

"What do you think happened to Jim?" I asked.

"I don't know. But I never would have expected him to leave suddenly like that. Too many people depend on him, and he was the kind of man who liked being depended on. I think it made him feel wanted. He needed that sense of helping others.

But maybe he just decided he'd done as much as he could around here and moved on to somewhere else."

"As in joining Doctors Without Borders, entering a religious order, living on the beach at Malibu? What are we talking about here?"

She seemed flustered. "I don't know where he'd go, but I'm sure he would never stop helping people."

"Didn't Jim have any flaws?" I asked, a little of my frustration at his flattering depictions by the women he had loved and left coming out in my voice.

Maggie stopped to think. "Well, Jim considered himself to be a good man, and sometimes you could sort of tell he was a little stuck on himself."

"A caped crusader complex."

She seemed offended by my flippant depiction of her boss and former lover.

"He really did help a lot of people," she said primly, and opened the door to the examining room as a clear indication that it was time for me to leave.

As I left, I wondered if there had been at least one person he hadn't helped and who had decided to get even.

CHAPTER 9

I've never known a wife beater. Oh, sure, I've probably had drinks and shot pool with plenty of them over the years; any woman who's gotten to know a cross section of the general male population has probably done that. But I've never actually known that they got their kicks by hitting women. That made me more than a little curious about Jed Turlow. I could have passed his name along to Jack and let him question the guy, but I wanted to check him out for myself. I'd been an M.P. long enough to be aware that when it really matters, you can't tell much by looking at people. Oh, sure, the general rowdies are pretty easy to spot in any crowd, but the really black-hearted guys more often than not have the open face of the neighbor boy next door. I was curious as to which category Turlow fell into. Would he be an obvious jerk or someone more subtle, someone who would resort to cold-blooded murder?

I stopped off at my condo for a quick lunch of cottage cheese and pineapple. I'd gotten used to a vegetarian diet during my time at the yoga center, and although it wasn't a matter of principle to me, I generally kept it up. I was washing it all down with a glass of water when my cell phone rang. Usually I let voicemail pick up; that way I can decide whether I want to call back and plan the conversation out in advance. You get into less trouble when you work from a script. But I figured that this might be related to Dr. Jim and I should pick up.

"It's Dianne Schianno," the caller said in response to my

hello. "I just talked to the caretaker of our place up on the lake."

"And?"

"He doesn't know anything about the house needing a new roof. In fact, he hasn't talked to Jim in several months."

I heard the worry in her voice. I wasn't sure whether she was bothered by the loss of the ten thousand dollars or Jim's lying to her. I had a feeling it was the second. Because if Jim had lied to her, she knew he must have been truly desperate.

There was a long moment of silence. I decided I was expected to fill in with a question.

"So why do you think your husband wanted ten thousand dollars?"

"I have no idea. The only thing I can think of is that he's gotten involved with a woman who needed rescuing and the money was going to help her."

"Could that also be why he disappeared?"

"You mean could he have done the same thing he did with me? Run off to another part of the country in order to help her escape an abusive husband?"

"Isn't that possible?"

She stopped to think about it. "I can believe he would leave Lauren or me in order to do that, but I don't think he would desert his sons even to save an abused woman. In fact, I don't really believe he would take money from our joint account to help another woman. We're not that well off. He knows we need the money for the boys' education."

"Maybe he plans to come back and repay it once he gets her relocated."

"Possibly."

"But you don't know of anyone he was planning to help in that way?"

"As I told you, he never told me any specifics about his . . . projects."

I told her I would keep checking into things and hung up. I went into my bedroom, wondering whether the woman Harry Link had seen showing off her charms down by the beach could have been the next candidate for Dr. Jim's special brand of healing. If she was, it didn't explain why Harry had seen her coming back by herself carrying a surfboard, or why the doctor's car was still at the beach the next day.

I went into my closet and hauled out a pair of cargo shorts and a T-shirt. I substituted them for my usual uniform of jeans and denim shirt. I covered my spiky hair with a baseball cap I'd gotten at a recent walk-a-thon the chamber of commerce had coerced me into underwriting. I looked in the mirror and decided that as long as someone didn't look too closely, I could pass for a normal suburban woman who was taking on a home repair project.

I went downstairs and got in my car. I'd already checked the phone book. There was only one lumberyard in the area Maggie had mentioned. About forty minutes later I managed to find Superior Lumber tucked away in an industrial park on the edge of North Berwick. There was a modern-looking store in the front that catered to the retail trade, but behind it were a couple of large gray sheds forming a yard where the lumber was stored. Aside from a trio of pickup trucks in the parking lot, things seemed pretty quiet.

I went into the store, plastered what I hoped was a pleasant smile on my face, and asked the senior citizen manning the cash register where I could find Jed Turlow.

"He's out back in the yard," the man answered. "But maybe I can help you."

I shook my head. "I've already talked to Jed about what I want, so I need to see him."

The man nodded doubtfully, as if no one really needed to see Jed, then he pointed toward the rear of the store.

"You'll find the door back there. It leads right out to the yard."

I hesitated. "I've never met Jed. What does he look like?"

The man smiled. "It's not very crowded out back. Jed will be the only guy wearing a shirt like this," he said, puffing his chest out to show the "Superior Lumber" name.

I nodded my thanks and followed his directions. Along the way I stopped at a bin holding three-foot long dowels of various thicknesses. I picked a lightweight one that snapped like a rapier when I whipped it back and forth in the air. I'd have rather had a police baton, but this would be less conspicuous.

Out in the lumberyard I glanced around without seeing anyone wearing an official shirt. A couple of guys close to the door were pulling out lengths of lumber, but they appeared to be customers. I headed toward the back of the sheds, switching the dowel in front of me like a blind man checking for obstacles. As I went around the corner, I almost ran into Jed Turlow standing right in front of me.

He was bending over, searching through a bin of woods scraps. When he heard me, he quickly turned and straightened, embarrassed to be seen in such an awkward position. He was an inch or two shorter than I am but solidly built with broad shoulders. He had black hair, and either had forgotten to shave or purposely cultivated dark stubble, probably on the mistaken notion that it made him look like a bad-boy fashion model rather than a derelict. He stared at me for a moment then smiled.

"You shouldn't be back here. You could get hurt."

"Oh, sorry," I said, trying to look properly helpless. "I thought this area was open to the public."

His smile twisted into a leer. "You have to be careful in a place like this."

I glanced around me and acted nervous, as if danger was lurking behind the racks of two-by-fours and plywood. That made him smile even more. As a boy he'd probably enjoyed bringing worms and mice to school to frighten the girls.

"Are you Jed Turlow?" I asked.

"At your service. How can I help you?"

He took a step closer, invading my personal space. I stepped back, pretending to stumble. I wanted him to be as off guard as possible.

"I was just wondering if you could tell me where Dr. Schianno is?"

A bewildered expression passed over his face, soon replaced by a snarl.

"Who the hell are you?"

"Oh, that's a real long story," I said, lightly. "But if you can tell me where he is, I'll be on my way."

He stepped closer; this time I glided backwards, staying out of arm's reach.

"I asked you a question, lady."

"I asked you one, too," I said, trying to sound cordial. "And mine is a lot more important, because it involves a missing person."

"What are you talking about?"

"Dr. Jim Schianno, the doctor you threatened because he helped your wife escape from your abuse, is missing. I thought maybe you could tell me what happened to him."

He was about to take another step toward me when he stopped.

"Are you from the police?"

"No. I'm a friend of the doctor's fiancée. She's trying to find him."

"Yeah, well, I don't know what happened to that bastard, and I don't care," he said, continuing toward me. I slid back another step. I took a quick glance around. The other men who had been in the lumberyard had disappeared.

"And what about your wife? Do you know where she is?"

That really wasn't a question to which I needed an answer. Admittedly, I was stepping over the line into gratuitous taunting.

"I don't know and I don't care. Like I told that doctor when he came around, I've got another girlfriend now."

"Gee," I said, "somehow you don't strike me as the kind of guy who would let his wife leave with a good-bye and good luck."

"What kind of guy do I seem like?" he asked with a nasty grin.

"Oh, the kind who probably makes up for his inadequacies in the bedroom by using his fists."

That seemed to provoke him. His nostrils flared, and he started to take another step toward me. Before his foot hit the ground, I whipped the dowel across my body and hit him a glancing blow on the side of the head about an inch away from his left eye. He stopped in his tracks and put his hand up to the side of his head.

"What the hell . . ."

Before he could say more, I backhanded him with the dowel across the nose. He fell back a step and covered his face. When he took his hands away I could see that his nose was turning a bright red and his eyes had begun to water. In my experience there's nothing like hitting someone in the nose to get him to lose his temper. A little blood would have been even better, but there's only so much you can do with a quarter-inch dowel.

He took a deep breath, and I could see that something switched on in his mind. A stiff smile was fixed on his face as if he was already imagining what he was going to do to me. He took a quick look and saw that no one was around.

He smiled. "Like I said, a lot of accidents happen in a lumberyard."

I nodded and shifted my weight subtly toward my good hip. He charged directly at me. At the last moment, I held the dowel in front of me like a sword. As I had expected, the dowel hit him in the chest and snapped, leaving me with about a third of it in my hand broken off into a sharp point. I quickly stepped to one side, shifting to my bad hip, and as Jed went rushing past me, I stuck my right foot out. He tripped and ended up face down on the ground.

As he rolled over and began to get up, I came down on the center of his chest with my left knee and shoved the sharp end of the stick under his chin. A red misty curtain descended. How long it went on, I'm not certain, but his squawking and thrashing finally brought me back. I saw a thin stream of red running through the stubble on Jed's neck. His head was pushed back as far as he could get it, but that hadn't been far enough. When I pulled it out, I estimated that the point of the stick had been shoved a good quarter inch into the fat under his chin.

"You're a crazy bitch," he said, now that he could talk again without pain.

"How about you tell me when you saw Dr. Jim last?"

"I'm going to sue you," he said, sticking his hand under his chin and blanching when he saw the blood.

"No, you're not. Because no one is around, and I'll tell the police you attacked me. Who do you think they're more likely to believe?"

"Get off me," he demanded, trying to roll out from under me. I clamped my legs tighter, feeling the pleasant sensation of his ribs bending inward.

"You'd better talk to me."

Instead he reached up and tried to push me off of him. He still didn't really believe a woman could hurt him. I shoved the stick in the back of my shorts, and reached forward with my right hand.

In adolescence, when lucky girls were busy growing large breasts, I was developing large hands. My father would frequently wonder where I had inherited what he called my farm-boy hands. "Must be from your mother's side," he would say sadly. I'd usually make some reply that they must have come from somebody on her side, because nobody related to him had ever earned an honest living. That would usually get me a boring lecture on how people who labor with their minds are working just as hard as those who bend their backs. Following my father's example, my brothers would say that I had hands like catchers' mitts. This was something of an exaggeration, although they were wide with long strong fingers and prominent knuckles. Many a drunken soldier had learned they could be put to good use.

I reached down with my left and pulled Jed's hand away from his chin, then I put my right on his neck spanning from one side to the other and began to tighten on the arteries, cutting off the blood supply to his brain. He reached up to try to pull my hand away, but I had the advantage of position and leaned into him.

"In a few seconds you're head is going to feel like it's going to pop. Then you'll black out, and there's no way for you to know how long I'll keep you blacked out. Maybe so long that people will think you've had a debilitating stroke. Wouldn't that be a shame? Nursing home, here I come. When you're ready to tell me when you saw Schianno last, nod your head. But you'd better make it soon before you lose consciousness."

His face turned an alarming shade of red, and blood from his chin began running down the back of my hand. I released my grip for an instant, then tightened again. I didn't want him unconscious, but I had to keep up the pressure until his fear overrode his rage. His eyes began to bulge, and I was afraid that he'd black out before I got an answer. Suddenly his head began to bob frantically. I released my grip.

"Talk," I said.

"He came to see me here," Turlow said in a raspy voice. "He said that if I tried to find my wife or threatened her or him in any way, he'd go to the police. He said she was ready to testify against me, and that he'd back her up with medical evidence."

"When was this?"

"Three weeks ago, I guess."

"And you haven't seen him since then?"

"I told you no. Now get off me."

He started to struggle. I slid back a little to get a better angle, then rammed the heel of my hand under his sore chin as hard as I could. I heard his jaw snap shut and watched his eyes roll up into his head. He wasn't badly hurt. By the time I got off him his eyelids were starting to flicker, and I knew that he'd be conscious again in a few minutes. That was my cue to leave. I bent over him, not sure whether he could hear me.

"You were right. A lot of accidents happen in a lumberyard," I whispered in his ear.

On the way out, I dropped my piece of bloody dowel back in the bin, although I doubted whether anyone would want to buy it.

CHAPTER 10

After leaving the lumberyard, I drove back home. Then I went down to the beach for my afternoon walk. I decided to start by heading north for the usual three miles. It was a clear day with warm sunshine that turned the ocean a deep blue. But the breeze hitting my face was stiff and cold enough to catch my attention as I headed up the beach.

I tried to visualize the breeze whistling through my head, blowing away all my tension. It didn't work. I was too worried about what I'd done to Jed Turlow. Not just because of what had happened, but because I hadn't been in full control when I'd acted. I've had these temporary periods of blind rage ever since I left the military; something would snap and I'd feel like another person had taken over my body. Ever since I was a kid, I've had what I thought of as a bad temper, but since leaving the Army, I'd begun to suspect that these rages were a symptom of something deeper. My time as an M.P. and my yoga training had helped me control the paroxysms of anger, but clearly the underlying cause was still there: a source of strength because it made me fearless, a source of weakness because of its unpredictability.

I also had no illusions that what I had done would make Turlow any less dangerous to women. In fact by humiliating the man, I had made him more likely to beat his girlfriend or any other unfortunate female who crossed his path. A guy like that, who didn't realize he had a problem, would never seek help.

Killing him was probably the only solution. Fortunately, that wasn't my job.

The only satisfaction I took away from the confrontation was that I could now be relatively certain he hadn't been involved in Dr. Jim's disappearance. He'd said as much, and Turlow didn't strike me as a good liar. He liked to brag about being a bully. I also doubted that he had the patience to work out an elaborate murder plan. If Turlow killed anyone, it would be on the spur of the moment, in a wild fit of fury—not unlike myself. Although I figured I had the patience to plan out a murder, too, if necessary.

The problem with dropping Turlow from my list of suspects was that it left me with no list at all. Since I hadn't been able to get Maggie to give me the names of the women who had benefited from Dr. Jim's extra-special medical care, my investigation had pretty much come to a standstill.

I supposed I could always go back to Maggie and lean harder on her for the information, but I had a feeling that Jim's disappearance wasn't linked to one of his special female patients. Since his separation, he'd apparently pretty much confined his romantic entanglements to Maggie and then Lauren. Of course, some sneaking around on the side could have gone undetected. However, his obvious state of anxiety during the week before his disappearance was new, according to Maggie, Lauren, and his wife. So I figured it must have come from a source other than his normal philandering, which had never been the cause of any concern to him in the past. And why the desperate need for ten thousand dollars? Maybe it was another one of his rescue missions or maybe it was something else. I had no idea.

I brooded on the money angle until I reached the end of my three miles. I turned around, putting the ocean on my left and heading to the south, carefully stepping in my own footprints. I tried practicing a walking meditation, concentrating on the feeling as my foot hit the wet sand. But my mind stubbornly kept returning to the investigation. I was halfway back to the car when I finally admitted I couldn't see any way to proceed without more evidence. If Dr. Jim was alive, maybe he would contact someone; if he was dead, possibly his body would still turn up. But as things stood right now, I'd have to tell Lauren that I'd accomplished all I could. Even though I'd done more than I had promised her, I felt a little guilty about not being able to help her more.

I paused for a moment to be honest with myself. I didn't really feel guilty because I couldn't help Lauren more. What bothered me was that I couldn't do more to help Dr. Jim. If I were certain he was fine and happily helping another victim of male brutality, I'd have walked away from this case without hesitation, but that wasn't the way it felt to me. And I thought I owed him my best effort. After all, he had done the same for me.

Lauren had given me her cell phone number and urged me to call her whenever I had anything to report. Even though what I had to tell her would be that we had reached the end of the road, she deserved to know. But my fears told me this was going to be another difficult human interaction meant to be delayed as long as possible.

Instead of calling her, when I got back home I cleaned the living room from top to bottom, then I took everything out of the kitchen cabinets and gave them a good wiping out with a damp sponge. Not that any of this needed to be done. I'd cleaned the entire area thoroughly only three days before. I've found that when I need to relax, mindless tasks work better than pills. I suspected that was one of the reasons the military put so much emphasis on routine housekeeping in basic training. When I was done, I read for a while and watched the local news to see if there was anything more about Dr. Jim, which there wasn't; then I ate some breakfast cereal. A light meal was all I'd allow myself on a teaching night.

I checked the clock. It was five-thirty. Lauren had told me that she got home by five. If I put it off any longer, I wouldn't be able to call until after nine. A disturbing conversation that late at night might prevent me from sleeping. Better to do it now, while I still had time to get my mind back under control.

I punched in Lauren's number.

"What have you found out?" she asked me excitedly after we'd said hello.

I gave her a concise summary of what I'd discovered. I started by telling her about meeting Harry Link at the beach, and his account of seeing a naked woman there that same evening.

"But Jim wasn't with her, was he?" Lauren asked in a shaky voice, worried that she had been betrayed.

"Not as far as I know. His car was there, but Link didn't see any sign of Dr. Jim."

"Do you think Jim was there to meet her?"

"Hard to say. It could have been a coincidence. Some folks like to get in some last minute surfing in the fall, but it is a little odd to be doing it so late in the day."

I told her about Dianne Schianno's story of how she met her husband and gave Lauren her interpretation of his numerous affairs.

"But that just proves what a nice guy he is," Lauren said. "He saved Dianne from a terrible man, and he's helped other women who were in trouble."

"He's also had romantic relationships with them."

There was a long silence before she spoke.

"Are you suggesting that's the kind of relationship I had with Jim? Because that wouldn't be true. He really loved me. I wasn't some kind of charity project. I'm perfectly capable of taking care of myself."

I thought of her waif-like looks and the series of failed relationships with older men she had told Karen about. In her own mind, she might be a tower of strength; reality seemed less impressive.

Ignoring her comment, I went on to tell her about Jed Turlow. I gave her a somewhat expurgated account of my encounter with him. No need to reveal too much about myself.

"Couldn't he have done something to Jim? He certainly sounds like a violent man."

"He is, and he may have had a motive. But I think if he was going to act on it, he would have done so sooner. His wife disappeared several weeks before Jim did."

"Maybe he needed time to plot his revenge."

I told her that Jed had quickly written off his wife and didn't strike me as much of a plotter. However, under pressure from Lauren I admitted that he couldn't be totally eliminated as a suspect. Then I told her about the mysterious ten thousand that Jim had taken from the joint bank account he had with his wife, and the fact that both Maggie and his wife had noticed a dramatic change in Dr. Jim's mood over the past week or so. Again, Lauren was silent for so long that I finally prompted her.

"You also mentioned that Dr. Jim's mood seemed different over that time."

"I thought so," she said hesitantly.

"Do you have any idea why he would have an urgent need for that much money?"

"Maybe he was going to help another woman."

"Possibly. Although his wife didn't think he'd take money from their joint account to do that. Can you think of any other reason he might have for needing so much cash right away?"

"No."

"Did he owe anyone money?"

"He didn't gamble or do drugs," she said defensively.

"It wouldn't have to be anything like that. Maybe he played the stock market or was involved in some kind of business where he needed money quickly to close a deal."

"You didn't know Jim. He didn't care about money. I think he just put whatever he had in the bank."

I wished people would stop telling me that I didn't know the guy. Especially when the people telling me seemed to have a less realistic picture of him than I did. But I had to admit that on brief acquaintance, Jim hadn't struck me as a smooth financial operator. I continued through my mental checklist of possible reasons why someone would be under pressure to come up with a large sum of cash.

"Could he have done anything wrong?"

"What do you mean?"

"I was thinking of something that might have led to black-mail."

"I told you Jim was a decent man," she replied slowly.

The words were what I had expected, but the tone seemed to be lacking in complete conviction, as if something might have occurred to Lauren.

"Have you got an idea?" I asked.

"There's something I have to do," she said abruptly. "I have to go now."

"Wait, why don't you tell me what's on your mind? Maybe I can help you."

"Look, you've helped me enough, and I know helping isn't really your thing. I appreciate everything you've done, but from now on I'll take care of this by myself."

Her critical dig at my lack of altruism annoyed me. "Fine," I said curtly.

I'm not sure whether I would have asked her to call me if she needed any further assistance, because she had hung up before I even had a chance to think about it.

★ ★ ★ ★ ★

I pulled into the yoga studio parking lot at six-thirty and walked up to the door.

"Are you Ali Randall?" a nervous voice asked from the shadows.

I spun to my left, adrenaline rushing into my system. He moved toward me into the light. A very tall, very thin, young guy stared down at the sidewalk as if afraid to look me in the face. He had on a T-shirt and a pair of chinos that seemed barely able to stay up on his skinny hips.

"Who are you?" I asked angrily.

I didn't like being surprised, and I was mad with myself for not being present enough in the moment to have spotted him, my conversation with Lauren still being on my mind.

"My name's Charlie Ross. Ananda sent me."

"Why?"

He peeked up at my face as if it was the sun on a bright day and he was afraid of burning his retina.

"Ananda thought that maybe you'd give me a job."

"Let's go upstairs," I said. I unlocked the door and marched up the stairs, not much caring whether he followed me or not.

When we got to the studio, I turned on the light and took a seat on one of the benches in the lobby. The boy was a few steps behind me. When he came into the lobby I motioned him toward the bench on the other side of the room. I didn't know him well enough to bring him into my small office where I'd have less room to maneuver if it became necessary. Since he was a lightweight, I figured I had a better than even chance in the open lobby if it came to trouble. He was probably safe if he came from Ananda, but it pays to be wary.

"How do you know Ananda?" I asked.

"I spent some time at the Savasana Center. I'm a registered yoga teacher."

A little pride came into his voice with the last sentence. Ananda was the person who ran the yoga center I'd lived in. A bald-headed guy of indeterminate age, I'd suspected that, like Izzy, he had a checkered past in which he'd done some things he wasn't proud of. I'd asked Anandaa few questions about what he had been involved in before setting up the center and had always been put off with jokes or vague answers. He was also the master of an eclectic brand of martial arts he claimed to have put together himself during his years in the Orient. I'd sparred with him a few times and learned a lot. Sparring had also told me something about his background. His teaching wasn't for kids. It wasn't even for guys who wanted to work their way up through a system of belts and compete in martial arts as a sport. It was for people who wanted to disable or kill.

I'd never known him to do anything without a reason either in the training room or outside of it, so I suspected that there had been a purpose in his sending Charlie to me. That didn't make me like the idea any better.

"Why did Ananda tell you to come to me?"

The kid shrugged.

A shrug can mean a lot of things. Maybe he didn't want to tell me, or perhaps he thought it was so obvious, I should have figured it out for myself. A more likely possibility was that he didn't know himself. Ananda gave orders, and you obeyed. If you asked questions, you were greeted with silence or Zen-like conundrums that made you wish you hadn't bothered. Ananda believed that eventually you would understand the purpose of his orders. If you didn't, it was because you weren't ready to know.

When he'd ordered me out of the center, I'd been bitter, resentful, and frightened. I'd challenged him and received what was actually one of his clearer explanations: a man who no longer needs a crutch to walk doesn't carry it around with him.

I'd pointed out that it should be my decision whether I was ready to walk on my own or not, but he'd merely smiled and nodded toward the door. I'd hobbled out on my bad hip thinking that if anyone needed a crutch, I certainly did.

"Did Ananda tell you to say anything to me?"

Charlie licked his lips. "He said I should tell you that one learns by teaching."

Whoop-de-do, I thought. Another wise saying of the East. I was tempted to get on the phone and call Ananda and tell him I was barely holding it together on my own; I certainly didn't need a kid to look after. But I knew that even if I was fortunate enough to get through to him, all I'd hear was another piece of fortune cookie wisdom.

"Do you want to teach yoga here?" I finally asked.

He nodded with some enthusiasm.

"You'll have to qualify. Even then, I'll only be able to start you out with one class a week. That won't be anywhere near enough to live on."

"I've got a job stacking shelves at the Hannaford's Supermarket up Route 1."

"Do you have a place to stay?"

"I've got a small apartment here in town."

I nodded, liking the kid better. At least he had established himself before showing up on my front door. If I had to be his teacher, so be it. At least I didn't have to be his primary means of support.

Julie walked into the room. She taught the class in the big room, while my less well-attended class was in the smaller one. She gave me her professional smile and kept it on her face as her glance passed quickly over Charlie. To give the boy credit, he quickly looked at Julie's face then returned his eyes to the floor without engaging in any lustful ogling. That gave me an idea.

"Julie, Charlie is a yoga teacher, and I'm thinking about giving him one of my classes. Could he sit in on your class tonight to see how things are done? If you have time right now, maybe the two of you could even work out a plan to team-teach. That way you could observe him as he leads the class through a couple of postures."

A momentary hint of annoyance flickered behind Julie's eyes, but the smile didn't dip.

"Sure," she said. She put her hand out to him. "I'm Julie Sawyer."

Charlie tentatively took her hand in his as if he wasn't familiar with the custom. "Charlie Ross," he mumbled.

"Well, let's go into the practice room, Charlie, and see what we can work out for tonight," Julie said cheerfully. She glanced at me.

I guiltily avoided her eyes. But really, people with all that spunk should expect to be imposed upon by those of us who have to carefully measure out our energy to survive the day.

CHAPTER 11

The students for Julie's class and my own began tromping up the stairs at about ten to seven. Julie's class usually numbered fifteen, the maximum the front room will comfortably hold. Most of them are in their twenties to early thirties with a few older women in good condition. My class was much smaller and more of a mixed bag. The number varied from five to seven depending on the phase of the moon. Tonight as I sat in the Half-Lotus checking over my plans for the class and looking out across the darkened room, I counted five. Two were heavyset women of late middle age who worked hard to challenge their limitations. Two were thin women with nervous dispositions, one of whom never came to class without wearing her pearls and a diamond encrusted watch. I worried that some day during class she would either choke herself or slit her wrist. The fifth student was a heavyset man, George Wright, who claimed to have serious issues with his back. Gray-haired and charming in an old-fashioned, courtly sort of way, he tended to be a bit chattier than I liked, but he helped to relax the two nervous women with his gallant compliments and endless small talk.

Just as I was about to begin—I'd even gone so far as to close the door—it opened with a bang and Sarah Contell came staggering in. She was carrying her yoga mat, a cushion, an eye bag, a bottle of water, and her metal cane, which she managed to get caught in the door, resulting in everything else falling on the floor.

I climbed to my feet as quickly as I could and went over to help her before George got involved and prolonged the matter even further. Sarah always carried the cane into class, although I'd frequently seen her walk briskly across the parking lot to her car swinging the cane as if it were a prop for her tap dance routine. Her problem always seemed to worsen when she saw me. I suspected she used the cane as an attempt to establish some kind of shared tie between us, a relationship I was determined to avoid.

As I bent down to get the last of the items arranged for her on the floor around her mat, she leaned over and whispered in my ear, "My hip is bothering me a great deal tonight, my dear, so perhaps you won't work that area too hard."

I slapped her solidly on the shoulder. "Remember, Sarah, from those who have had much taken, much more will be asked."

A puzzled expression passed over her face, and I returned to the front of the room smiling to myself. After fifteen minutes of stretching warm-ups, I led the class through ten minutes of Vinyasa, a series of flowing movements that went from posture to posture, at a slow but steady pace. It raises the heart rate gradually and at the same time serves to focus the mind, proving the point that yoga is meditation in motion.

Then we moved on to a series of postures that got into various areas of the back, which I knew George would particularly appreciate despite his groans. Next we did a sequence that went from Downward Dog to the Pigeon posture. I held the Pigeon for a long time because it gets deeply into the hips, an area I need to stretch. Sarah might have been unhappy, but when I glanced up she was gamely doing it along with everyone else. We concluded with a number of postures on the floor meant to stretch the spine, and by the time I directed them into the Corpse posture for the last ten minutes of the class I was feeling the most relaxed I had been all day. As I sat in the Half-Lotus and looked out over them lying on their backs, covered in blankets, with their hands facing upward at their sides, I found my thoughts wandering away from my breath.

Savasana truly is the posture of a corpse. We have a natural tendency to roll onto our stomachs for safety because it protects our major internal organs from harm. As I'd learned in the Army, a person who is lying on his back is either dead or incapacitated. That bit of information I'd gotten from a captain whose checkered military career had started out in the infantry before he transferred into the military police.

My mind went back to the first time we'd met. My partner and I had been called out to a bar on base where there was a report of a minor disturbance. By the time we got there the trouble had spread, and there were at least ten soldiers involved in a number of separate fights. The biggest one was in the middle of the room where six guys were flailing away rather ineffectually at each other. Then there were two pairs of guys going at it with more purpose in opposite corners of the room. We called for backup and decided to start by breaking up the smaller fights because the participants seemed more serious. My partner headed over to the two guys going at it on the right side of the room, and I went to the left.

My pair didn't seem to be having a very fair fight. The bigger of the two had his opponent pinned on top of a wooden table and was pounding his head up and down. I shouted out a warning that I was an M.P., then reached around the big guy with both arms and dragged him off his opponent. He came away with surprising ease. I saw why when he turned to face me. Blood was running down the side of his face and into his right eye from a jagged wound at the hairline. I guessed the smaller guy was tougher than he looked. He proved it by bounding off the table, seeming none the worse for having his head repeatedly concussed. They were about to go back at it again, so in a clear but nonbelligerent voice I warned them not to do so.

Although female M.P.s are generally smaller and have less command presence in a bar brawl situation, they have the advantage of not provoking the "I'm-tougher-than-you-are" sort of response that a male M.P. might bring out in already wired guys. The drawback is that when men drink too much their libido also rises to the surface and the sight of a female can also suggest a possible victim. I could see by the malicious smirk on the smaller man's face that this was happening now. I pegged him as a guy who probably had a long list of sexual assaults in his past. He glanced over at the bigger guy, and I could see the thought pass like telepathy. The big guy wiped the blood off his face onto his sleeve and gave a small nod. I got a sinking feeling that perhaps these two guys were buddies who'd had a temporary falling out and had just decided to reconcile in the interest of committing another crime. It's always bad when it turns out the opponents are friends, because once they decide to play nice, the dynamics of the conflict change.

They began moving toward me. They were in fatigue uniforms, so their names were sewn on the front of their shirts. I said both names clearly to let them know they'd be held responsible for their behavior and ordered them to stand still. That didn't seem to make an impression. From the gleam in their eyes and their loose-limbed walk, it was clear both were at the stage of drunkenness where they were able to act but unable to calculate the consequences of their actions, making them particularly dangerous.

I looked across the room, and saw that my partner was fully engaged in handling his own fight. His back was toward me, and he had no idea of the situation I was confronting. I risked a glance over my shoulder and saw that behind me was a long hall leading to the restrooms. The men were coming at me slowly, staying far enough apart that I couldn't get around them, herding me toward the hallway. I wasn't going to let them get me down there. Once they did what they planned, they might realize I could easily identify them in the closed community of a military base and decide their only option was to kill me. If they were going to do that, it would have to happen out here where everyone could see, including my partner if he ever decided to turn around.

I took the baton off my belt, extended it to its full two-foot length, and began considering which one to lay out first. The big guy was on my right, and since I'm right-handed, it made sense to take him down and try to backhand the smaller guy as he moved in. The only problem was that the big guy was really big, around six-three and two hundred fifty pounds with a head that looked as hard as a cinder block. I wasn't sure that one blow would bring him down, even though blood was still running down his forehead, and I doubted I'd have time for a second shot before the little guy would be on me. If I tried to hit the smaller guy first, I'd be reaching across my body and the big guy might be able to pin my arm to my chest.

I had just flipped a mental coin and planted my feet solidly on the floor, hoping to hit the big guy hard enough the first time to scramble his senses when a deep, rumbling voice bellowed, "What's going on here?"

I didn't look over to see where the question came from, but the big guy did. As he turned his attention to the source of the noise, I swung across my body in a modified batter's swing and clouted the smaller guy on the side of the head. He stood there for a moment with a surprised expression on his face, then collapsed to the floor like a marionette whose strings had been cut. The big guy noticed his friend fall. He gave a roar, and with surprising speed got up on the balls of his feet ready to charge me. I was hoping to spin out of the way and tap him hard on the back of the head as he went past. But before he could move, there was a blur of motion to my right, and suddenly he was flying through the air. He crashed into the wall ten feet away hard enough to dent the wallboard and loosen the light fixture, which came down on his head. Before he could come to his senses, a bear of a man wearing captain's bars had rolled him onto his belly and slapped cuffs on him.

Before straightening up, the captain put two fingers on the neck of the smaller man. He glanced up at me.

"He's still alive. That's good. I hate all that paperwork when they don't make it."

He stood up. The captain wasn't any taller than I was, but he had a massive chest and arms. His hair was long, pushing at the limits of regulation, and although it had once been black, it was now liberally sprinkled with gray. I figured him for being in his late thirties, pretty young for a man but old for a captain.

He gave me a nod. "Guess I'm your new C.O." He glanced at my chest. "Good work, Randall."

"Thanks for your help, sir. I'm not sure how the situation would have gone without it."

He looked around the room, which seemed to have settled down of its own accord. The large fight in the center had ended in an exchange of verbal insults as everyone got exhausted, and my partner seemed to have settled down the two on his side of the room.

The captain gave me an appraising look. "I'd guess that you probably separated the two guys first."

I nodded.

He shook his head. "Always go in hard, Randall, especially if the big guy is winning. Put him down right away, then sort things out. Otherwise you never know when it will become an us-against-them kind of situation. And when there's two of them against one of us, the odds aren't good. Some company commanders might give you grief about cracking a few heads. I won't."

"I'll remember that, sir."

And I did. The situation came up a couple of other times, and I'd always gone in hard. I knew what he had said was true: not every C.O. would have backed up that kind of approach, but the captain always did. He said that the first duty of any commanding officer was to protect his people. Whether you do it by the book isn't nearly as important as keeping your people safe.

I pulled my mind back to the present, annoyed that I'd let my concentration drift away from my breath. I checked the clock with my penlight and saw it was time to end the class. I struck the little gong on the floor beside me three times and began taking my students through the steps to return to full consciousness. When everyone was upright in a seated position on the floor, I bowed to each of them and said "Namaste." I walked across the room and turned the lights up higher, then kept going, hoping to get safely into my office without being caught up in any small talk. Behind me I could hear George Wright keeping the women entertained, but before I could get through the lobby, Sarah Contell, bad hip suddenly forgotten, cut me off.

"Are you planning to do any more advertising?" she asked, peering up at me. "You know, a small business needs to get its name out there."

"I plan to start some advertising in a month or so," I said, at the same time trying to outflank her and make it into my office. She did a neat shuffle to her left and blocked my way.

"Putting flyers in people's mailboxes is a good idea, but it must be kind of expensive, paying someone to do all that door-to-door stuff."

I gave her a puzzled look. "I never put flyers in mailboxes."

"Well, somebody did," she replied. "It only had a few of the classes listed on it, but that's why I gave a call six weeks ago and decided to sign up. I'd never have known you were here except for that flyer."

"Well, maybe the Chamber of Commerce did something without telling me," I said, sure she had gotten it wrong. "I've received several calls from them since I joined, about their interest in supporting new small businesses."

Sarah shrugged doubtfully. "Anyway, if you do any promotions in the future, don't forget to include those of us who are loyal customers. Maybe you could do a coupon taking some money off a series of classes. You know, those of us on a fixed income can use every little bit of help we can get."

I nodded reluctantly. I'd seen Sarah leave the parking lot driving what appeared to be a rather new Lexus.

"I'll certainly take your idea into consideration," I replied, feinting to the left, then dodging past her on the right. My quick smile of triumph had disappeared from my face by the time I turned and said good-bye to her before closing the office door. I couldn't afford to antagonize such a loyal customer.

I sat in the office counting my breaths for ten minutes until I was reasonably certain all the students from both classes had left. But when I opened the door a crack and peered out, I saw Julie and Charlie lingering in the lobby, talking. I was tempted to softly close my door and return to counting, but decided I did have some minimal responsibilities as owner/manager of the studio. I walked out into the lobby.

"So how did it go, people?" I asked in what I hoped was a non-threatening voice.

"Fine," Julie said, giving me a smile that seemed more genuine than usual. She glanced over at Charlie and grinned. "I think Charlie will fit in fine here."

"Good," I said. Charlie was staring down at the floor and

didn't say anything, but there was a small, confident smile on his face that seemed to indicate agreement with Julie.

"Um, we were thinking," Julie began, "that maybe Charlie and I could teach together. For a while. I mean, until we start getting more students. I'm not sure there are enough right now to start adding classes."

Although I didn't care much for Julie telling me how to run my business, I had to admit she was right. If I added a class or two for Charlie, there was no guarantee there would be enough students for them to run.

"Okay. But I can't afford to pay two people to teach the same class. How would we handle the salaries?"

Julie's brow wrinkled as if she were considering a plan. I had a feeling this was just for show, and she'd already formulated her proposal.

"How about if you pay us one third more than I get alone? I'd be willing to split fifty-fifty with Charlie."

"So I pay you forty dollars for a class rather than thirty, then you and Charlie would each get twenty?"

She gave me one of her dazzling professional smiles and nodded.

"Would you be satisfied with that?" I asked Julie. "You'd end up with less."

"Sure. But to be honest, I sometimes find that teaching four classes a week leaves me pretty sore because I lead people through each exercise the same way you do. With Charlie on board, we can divide up the work, and it'll be a lot easier on me."

"Okay. Sounds fine. Is that plan all right with you, Charlie?"

He looked up briefly through long eyelashes and met my eyes. "Sounds good."

"Great," Julie added, turning and giving Charlie another smile. She got a nod in return.

I gave her a nod as well. She must have felt like she was surrounded by bobbleheads.

"Thanks for giving me the chance, Ali," Charlie said softly.

"I hope it works out," I replied in a neutral voice, letting him know that I was doing this mostly for Ananda.

"Charlie and I are going out to get a cup of coffee and talk about things," Julie said. "Would you like to come along?"

I felt the familiar surge of panic I get whenever people try to lasso me into a social situation. I took a deep breath to slow my heart rate before I replied.

"No, thanks. I have a couple of things to do yet around here."

"Okay," she said brightly, "maybe some other time." I thought I might have detected a note of relief in her voice.

Maybe the thought of trying to keep a conversation going with both Charlie and myself at the same time seemed daunting even to the exuberant Julie. More likely she was just being polite in asking me along, and I'd have been intruding on the development of their personal relationship.

As I watched them leave the studio together, Julie chirping happily about something and receiving not much in response from Charlie, it occurred to me that I really owed it to Julie to find out more about Charlie's past. I didn't think Ananda would saddle me with someone who was truly dangerous, but it would be nice to know how he had ended up at the Savasana Center. If his reason for being there was anything like mine, the center had been at the end of a rough patch of road.

I went back into my office, taking the payment box with me. I had actually been telling the truth about having some work to do. I had to reconcile the accounts and post the figures on the spreadsheet my accountant demanded I use for tax purposes. By the time I finished, it was nine o'clock. I was stretching my leg out to get some of the tightness out of my hip when I heard the downstairs door open. *Sloppy, sloppy, sloppy,* I muttered to myself. I always warned the teachers to keep the downstairs door locked if they were going to hang around to practice on their own, and here I was disobeying my own cardinal rule. Cornwall had a crime rate well below the national average, but that didn't mean crime never happened. People don't get killed on the average; they get killed for real, one by one. And I had no intention of being a victim.

I carefully slid open my lower right-hand desk drawer and took out the police baton I'd purchased over the Internet. I walked quickly across the room and waited by the side of the doorway with the baton poised, ready to give the intruder a sharp poke in the ribs. Striking blows are overrated. They take too long and give your opponent a chance to block with an arm. Try blocking a poke in the midsection or to the forehead. It isn't easy. And it can stun a person enough that you can then follow up with an unblocked head strike that puts him down.

The person climbing the stairs had almost reached the top by the time I was in position. I got set to follow through with a quick thrust that would have some force behind it.

"Ali," a familiar voice said, "if you're standing there ready to puncture my liver you might want to reconsider."

"Izzy?"

"One and the same," he said, stepping through the doorway. His eyes rested on the baton for a moment. "Guess it's a good thing I gave you some warning or I'd have a couple of cracked ribs."

"Even more warning would have been better. I don't need an adrenaline rush just before going home."

"I would have phoned, but I was passing by and decided to stop on impulse."

I waved him to a seat in the lobby and settled down across the way with my bad leg stretched out in front of me. I had my doubts about whether Izzy did anything on impulse.

"So what's up?" I asked.

"The truth is I was feeling guilty about our last conversation."

"Why's that?"

"I wasn't fully focused on you while we were talking."

"Because you had that rape victim on your mind. No need to apologize."

"So I thought that I'd stop by again to see how your investigation of Dr. Jim is going. This time you have my full attention."

I filled him in on what had happened. That included giving Izzy the unexpurgated version of my encounter with Jed Turlow in the lumberyard.

When I was done, he stared at the carpet for a long time.

"You don't think that what you did to Turlow might have been a little . . . extreme?"

I shrugged.

"It really isn't your job to go around punishing men who abuse their wives."

"I didn't do it because of that. I needed information, and that seemed to be the only way to get it."

"Sure you weren't getting back at him for what he did or for the things that have happened to you?"

I shook my head. "I'm not leading an army of vengeful females. I'm just one woman picking her way carefully through life. Sure, I had an emotionally distant father, a lover who lied to me, and I got wounded in what looks like a pretty pointless war. But I figure that puts me somewhere in the middle of the pack of abused women, not out in front. Others have had it a lot worse."

"People might say that what you did had some of the characteristics of sociopathic behavior."

"C'mon, Izzy, a female sociopath is just a woman who acts like your average man. If a guy had done that to Turlow under the same circumstances, you'd say he was a hero."

"I don't care about Turlow. I care about you. These outbursts of violence are still happening over two years after you came back. Sometimes I think that deep down you don't want to heal."

"Healing is overrated," I snapped, feeling my face get hot. "It's the kind of thing that cookie-cutter shrinks talk about who want everyone to fit into society without any rough edges. I'd rather be the way I am than end up a zombie."

"You've got to get past what happened to you."

"Get past it." I heard my voice become fierce. "That's what makes me what I am. If I get past it, there's nothing left. It's the best part of me."

I could see Izzy start to deny this, but then his jaw muscles tensed and no words came out. That's why I love Izzy. He's too honest to lie to me.

After a few moments he said, "There's a good band down at the Blackbird tonight. They play a lot of the old sixties stuff. I need a beer, and you could have a glass of water. It would probably do us both good. I could teach you how to swing dance."

"I think my swing dancing days are over," I said. "But that glass of water sounds really good."

We got to our feet and headed for the door. As I switched out the lights I heard Izzy say from in front of me going down the stairs, "Some of it may be the best part of you, Randall, but not all of it. You've got to sort out what to keep and what to let go."

I grunted. Easy for him to say.

CHAPTER 12

I slept well that night. Probably because Izzy did manage to drag me out on the floor for a couple of relatively slow swing dances. He ignored my reluctance to show off my handicap and said my tendency to favor one side over another made it appear that I had my own dancing style. I figured that was a charitable interpretation.

But although I got up in the morning in pretty good spirits, I found that by the time I had done my Sun Salutations and eaten breakfast, I was restless and edgy, much the way I'd been when I'd first come home from Iraq. Then I'd constantly felt like there was something I should be doing—something I desperately needed to do—but what it was remained just outside my range of consciousness. However, it was always there as a shadowy but constant mental torment, never allowing me a moment of complete peace.

This morning, before I fully realized it, I had paced back and forth across the living room so often, my hip was aching. I slumped into a chair and stretched my bad leg out in front of me. I decided to try becoming mindful. Mindfulness is a Buddhist practice in which you focus your thoughts on why you are presently experiencing a certain emotion. As I sat in the Half-Lotus and relaxed, closing my eyes softly and counting my breaths, I gradually realized what bothered me was something I wasn't doing—I was no longer involved in the investigation into Dr. Jim's disappearance. Although I had only been doing it for two days and hadn't invested much of my time, apparently I had put a lot of psychic energy into arriving at a solution.

When I asked myself why I felt such a sense of guilt at ending what was a rather minor commitment, it came home to me that this was the first time I'd taken on the burden of helping someone since I'd returned home. And I didn't want my first attempt to end in failure.

"See," I scolded myself, "you were right to be reluctant to get involved in someone else's life. This is what happens."

But involved I was. Whether my primary sense of responsibility was to Lauren or Dr. Jim, I couldn't tell, but I definitely wasn't feeling comfortable walking away from the matter.

There were two ways I could deal with this. I could force myself to stay out of it and hope that, over time, my sense of commitment would fade and eventually I'd be back to where I was a week ago. I wasn't certain that would be a good thing. The other way was to call Lauren and firmly tell her I wanted to continue helping her with the search for Dr. Jim. The risk there was that I would deepen my commitment, and we would still be unsuccessful, leading to more frustration. I checked in with my feelings and knew which course I needed to follow.

I called Lauren.

"Hi, Lauren," I said, struggling to sound bright and cheerful. "I wanted to check in on how things are going."

"Going with what?" Lauren responded.

"With our investigation into Jim's disappearance."

"It's not 'our' investigation," she said sharply. "I told you I didn't need your help."

I paused for a moment. She was so rude, it was like having a conversation with myself.

"Are you pursuing it?" I asked.

She sighed. "As pointless as it seems, I am."

"Why is it pointless?"

"Because I think it's going to turn out that Jim was a different person than I thought he was."

"What man isn't?" I was tempted to say, but I held my tongue.

Instead I asked, "In what way is he different than you thought?"

"I don't want to talk about it right now. Plus I have to work out a few more things first."

"Okay. Are you coming to Karen's class tonight?"

"I don't know," she said.

"I'd really like a chance to talk to you," I said gently.

"Yeah, whatever. I'm not sure I'll be able to make it."

I could only put on my kindly friend act for so long, and it had reached the breaking point.

"Look," I said. "If you don't show up in the studio tonight so I can talk to you, I'll be coming to your house. And if you're not home, I'm going to let Jack know that you're meddling in a police investigation. Do you understand?"

"I'm sorry I ever asked you for help," she shot back.

That makes two of us, I thought.

"Just make sure I see you tonight."

The phone went dead.

I sat by the sliding door to the deck and stared across the wetlands toward the row of houses along the shore. The mile distance shrank them to doll houses, neatly lined up just out of reach of high tide. Distance diminished everything eventually. Even the strongest emotion would eventually weaken as time took its gradual, diminishing toll. Lauren's feelings were still raw. Dr. Jim's disappearance was the end of the world to her, and she was clearly overreacting to the situation. But what had she meant by saying he was a different person than she thought he was?

My mind drifted. I was lying on an army bed with the captain, which was not the easiest thing for two rather large people.

After making love, we always struggled to arrange ourselves comfortably, twisting around until we were flesh to flesh rather than bone to bone. My head was resting on his chest and I was listening to the deep, steady beat of his heart. A hot, dry breeze blew through the one small window. I tried to imagine where that breeze had come from and pictured it travelling over waves of sand in the Sahara, across North Africa and through the Middle East until it crossed the Tigris and Euphrates to where we were at this one perfect moment. Two Americans in a faraway place and deeply in love: the romantic image made me smile. I felt like the heroine in a Hemingway novel. This was so different from everything I'd ever thought about in the suburbs of Boston. This was what real life was meant to be.

"What are you going to do when you get out of the Army?" I asked.

I heard his heart begin to beat more rapidly.

"Why do you ask?"

His voice was slow and unnaturally calm. I'd learned over time that this was the way he spoke when under stress. I felt the ominous rumble of the words through the ear that was on his chest as their meaning came into my mind through the other. I wondered which was more accurate.

"You told me in another year you'll have twenty in. That means you can retire. I was just wondering what you plan to do."

"I don't know."

"Do you think it's bad luck to talk about it?"

Some guys never talked about going home because they figured it was a jinx. With others, it was about all they talked about. What both sides had in common was that they really wanted to make it home because there was something waiting for them there. I was different. I never talked about going home because I didn't have a home to return to. I figured I'd just stay in the Army until I had a good reason to leave.

"No," the captain said, "I don't think about luck that way. Sometimes you're lucky and sometimes you're not, but I don't think you can do anything to change it. It happens the way it happens."

I nodded, rubbing my ear on his chest.

"So why don't you think about retiring then?"

"Because I don't have a clue what I'd do. I don't have much left back home. I've only lived in the States for about eight of the last twenty years. I'm Army more than I am American."

"You grew up in Nebraska. Maybe you want to go back there."

He laughed. "I barely stayed there long enough to finish high school. That's one place I know I won't be going." He paused for a moment. "And, you know, I don't really have any family."

He'd told me that he was divorced and hardly knew his two children. He still remembered them more as they had been eight years ago than as the high school and college students they had become.

"Maybe you could get to know them again," I said, using it more as a test than an actual suggestion.

"Too late. They'd never forgive me for neglecting them, for volunteering for overseas assignment when I could have stayed home. And they'd be right, because I didn't try to settle down and become much of a father to them."

I hiked myself up on one elbow so I could see his face. I ran my hand over the salt and pepper hair on his chest.

"You know my current hitch is up in a year. There's nothing to keep me in the Army. We could get out at about the same time and start a new life together."

He shook his head. "I'm too old for you. I could be your father if I'd gotten my high school girlfriend pregnant," he said with a grin.

"But you're not," I snapped. "And what difference does age

make anyway. We get along pretty well, don't you think?"

He smiled and ran his hand through my hair.

"We get along fine here. But this isn't the most normal of situations."

"No, it's a hell of a lot harder. So doesn't that mean things will be even easier if we are somewhere else? We don't have to move to Nebraska or even back to the States. I'll bet we could find work in Europe or anywhere in the world we wanted to be."

"That would be okay as far as it goes. But after a while you'd want to settle down and have a family. I tried that once. It didn't work for me."

"Just because you were a lousy father in your twenties doesn't mean you'd be as bad in your forties." I paused. "Anyway, I'm not so sure I'd ever want a family. From what I know about them, they can be pretty overrated."

The captain gave me a long look.

"You're too young to know yet what you want, Randall. Give yourself some time. You'll be rotating home in a few months. See how you feel when things get back to normal."

I leaned forward and kissed his neck.

"I know how I'm going to feel. The same way I do now, only then I'll be lonelier because you won't be around."

He smiled. "That's really sweet. But like I said, I'm not ready to think about it yet. You know, when you've been in the military as long as I have, you get out of the habit of making decisions about what to do with your life. Sure, every few years you have to decide whether to reenlist or not, but other than that you pretty much go where they send you, and do what you're told. You take it day-by-day and let the future worry about itself."

"You wouldn't reenlist, would you? They'd just send you back here."

"I haven't decided yet."

I slumped down on his chest, a wave of disappointment washing over me. I wanted to shout at him that this was the time to make a decision rather than letting life just happen to him. I wanted to tell him that we were a great couple and we shouldn't let what we had slip away. But I knew the captain well enough to realize he'd said all he had to say on the matter.

"You'll have your twenty in before I have to decide whether to reenlist. Will you at least let me know what you've decided to do, so I can make plans? Let me know no matter where you are or where I am?"

"I'll do that. I promise."

I relaxed. I knew he was a man who wouldn't lie to me.

And just like Lauren, I'd discovered the guy I loved was a different man than I thought he was.

I was still restless. I couldn't wait around and hope that Lauren was willing to tell me what she had discovered. I took out my phone and gave the police station a call. When I got through, I asked to speak with Jack. Fortunately he was there and available.

"Hi, Alison," he answered, sounding a bit more subdued than usual.

"Hey, Jack. I was wondering if any of your people have had a look around Dr. Jim's apartment."

"An officer got the super to let him inside the day he disappeared just to check that he wasn't lying there dead or incapacitated. But we haven't done a search. After all, we aren't even sure any crime has been committed. Theoretically, he could have decided to take off on a vacation without telling anyone."

"How likely do you think that is?" I asked.

"Not very. But even if he's run away for some reason, that isn't a crime in and of itself."

"He is a missing person."

118

"And we've got him officially listed that way. But we have no solid evidence of foul play."

"Right. But don't you think it's suspicious enough be looked into further?"

There was no answer. I wasn't sure what was wrong. I'm not very good at reading people, but even I could sense that something had changed in Jack's attitude toward me. There was a coolness in him I hadn't noticed before.

"Did you want something, Alison?" he asked.

"Yeah. I was going to ask for a favor. I wanted to know if it would be possible for me to take a look around Dr. Jim's apartment. I figured I might find something that would give me some idea as to where he's gone."

I heard a deep sigh on the other end of the line.

"I guess that's not a bad idea. Maybe you're right; we should put more effort into this case. I've been busy with a lot of other things. In the back of my mind, I suppose I've been assuming that he'd turn up eventually with some excuse involving a woman who was in trouble."

"It still might play out that way."

"Yeah. But I don't like the fact that he hasn't contacted his family at all. Why don't you meet me at his apartment in a half hour, and we'll see what we can find? He's at 145 High View."

"Thanks, Jack."

"Sure."

I hung up and took a deep breath. Something was wrong there. Jack was one of the few people who usually sounded happy to hear from me, but this time I had sensed some strain. That's what I hate about getting involved with people. Sooner or later everyone becomes a problem, then you have to expend a ton of effort working things out. I didn't have so much energy to spare.

Dr. Jim's new digs didn't compare very favorably with the place he'd shared with his wife and boys. The house was a big, rambling structure that once had been the gracious summer home of a wealthy Boston family; but somewhere along the way it had been divided up into six small condominiums intended as summer rentals. Since there wasn't much in the way of permanent rentals in Cornwall, when his wife had cast him out, Dr. Jim didn't have any choice but to become a tourist in his own town. And he'd clearly been forced to take what was left because his tiny bedroom-living room combination had a view of the parking lot. I wondered why he hadn't moved inland where he could have found cheaper, year-round rentals. My guess was that either he wanted to be near work or maybe, like me, he liked being able to walk on the beach whenever the mood hit him.

"This shouldn't take long," Jack said, surveying the place.

I nodded, hoping it wouldn't. Jack had greeted me with the restrained smile and polite manner you'd use with someone you didn't much like but couldn't be bothered to offend. I knew the expression. It was my usual one. I didn't know what his sudden problem was with me, but I make it a matter of principle never to ask. People seem to get around soon enough to telling you things you don't want to hear anyway.

"No computer," I said.

Jack nodded. "He probably used the one at work for medical things. I'll check with his wife to see if he had another one he left at home, or whether he had a laptop he normally carried with him."

While Jack searched through the clothes in the tiny closet, I checked the cheap dresser and bedside table. In the top dresser drawer, I came across his checkbook. He had been paying over two thousand a month during the summer for this vest pocket condo. I'll bet he'd wished his wife had waited until the off season to throw him out. There weren't a lot of other checks written. There was one for a hundred dollars made out to one of his sons. I wondered if that was a birthday gift. Not the most personal of presents, but maybe a wise choice when you're not home a lot to find out what they want. It had certainly been my father's approach with me.

The utilities must have been covered in the rent, because there were no household payments other than telephone. There were several checks to charities for amounts less than fifty dollars, credit card payments, a check for two hundred dollars made out to an auto body shop, a payment for an auto registration, and a number of checks written to "cash" in amounts under five hundred. All in all, nothing very surprising. I told Jack the news.

"Yeah. Nothing here either," Jack said, backing out of the closet. "He wasn't the kind of guy who left stuff in his pockets."

I walked over to the small kitchen area, which was little more than a counter with a stove, sink, and dishwasher built in. There were a few boxes of breakfast cereal in a closet, along with a loaf of bread, two cans of tuna fish, and some store-bought cookies. The refrigerator revealed a half-gallon of sour milk, which I dumped out, orange juice, some American cheese, and a half jar of mayo. There was nothing hidden in the sugar bowl I could discover by spooning through it.

"Other than breakfast and the occasional sandwich, I'd say Dr. Jim ate out or at Lauren's. He doesn't seem to have spent much time here," I said. "Certainly not enough to get his two thousand dollars worth."

Jack looked up from where he was peering under the bed with a pocket flashlight.

"Yeah. Well, you wouldn't expect anything different from a

guy in transition. He wasn't likely to put down roots here."

Jack got to his feet and took a final look around.

"I lived in a place like this for a while when my marriage broke up."

I'm never quite sure what to say when people suddenly bring up personal stuff like that. Do they want you to ignore it as a momentary lapse in good taste, or is it a hint that they'd like to tell you more about their lives?

"I didn't know you'd been married," I said, figuring it was safest to stick to the facts.

"It ended five years ago."

I looked at his gaunt face with the large brown eyes, the jutting cheekbones, and the curly dark hair. His face seemed even thinner than usual, and his expression more mournful.

"What happened?" I said, amazed that I had asked the question.

He shrugged. "She found someone that she liked better."

"That happens."

"Yeah."

I wasn't sure what I was supposed to say next. This had quickly gone beyond my usual scripted small talk.

"I saw you at the Blackbird last night," Jack said. He looked at the floor, trying to decide whether to say more. "You were with some guy."

"Yeah. He's sort of a friend and sort of a therapist."

Jack looked up at me, startled. "You go out on dates with your therapist? Is he out of the same school of unethical behavior as Dr. Jim?"

I smiled at that. "Izzy is sort of unconventional. But that wasn't a date. He just wanted me to get out and be around people more. I guess he figures that if I act like I'm having fun, then eventually I'll really be able to have fun. Pretense becomes the reality; must be some kind of behavioral therapy."

"How's that working for you?"

"Not real well so far."

Jack smiled. I figured he was just as happy I wasn't having a wonderful time with Izzy. I didn't break it to him that it wouldn't matter who I was with because I was always with myself. No reason to shatter his dreams.

"Is this investigating you're doing part of your therapy as well?"

"Maybe so. Izzy didn't suggest it to me, but I guess in a way it is. It's certainly forced me to do things I've been avoiding for a long time."

"Such as?"

"Getting involved in other people's lives."

"You have a narrow comfort zone for that kind of thing?" Jack asked.

I stretched my arms out a foot in front of me. "That's about where it ends."

Jack reached out and took my hands.

"Is that so painful?" he asked.

I forced myself to keep from pulling away. I began counting breaths and consciously relaxing my body. When my arms began to tremble, he released me.

"I guess it is," he said sadly.

"Sorry."

"Well," he said, consciously changing the subject. "Do you have any other ideas as to the whereabouts of Dr. Jim?"

"No. But Lauren has discovered something." I related her comment about Dr. Jim not being the man she thought he was.

"I guess we're not talking about an assumed identity here," Jack said.

"From her tone of voice, I think she meant that in some way he hadn't lived up to her picture of him."

"Maybe she found out he was cheating on her," Jack suggested.

"Could be. She wouldn't tell me what it was about."

"Maybe we should go talk to her right now."

I shook my head. "She seemed pretty spooked. I'm supposed to meet with her at the studio tonight. If what she has to say is relevant to the investigation, I'll let you know. Then you can decide if you need to talk to her."

Jack thought for a moment. "Okay, that will be all right. But if she does have any important information, you promise you'll let me know?"

"It's a promise."

I surveyed the apartment one last time.

"When is the landlord going to dump his stuff?" I asked.

"The rent's paid up to the end of the month. So it's safe until the end of next week. I guess his wife will have to decide what she wants to do with his things." Jack went over to the drawer that held Jim's checkbook and bills. He took them out and put an elastic band around them. "I think I'm going to take this stuff as evidence. I wouldn't want it to get lost in case this turns into a criminal investigation at some point."

We left the building and walked to our cars. Jack stopped by the front of his cruiser.

"If you ever need any help being out and around people again and your therapist can't make it, you can always give me a call. Even though I'm a cop, I know how to respect people's boundaries when I'm off duty."

I looked at him, not sure what to say.

He smiled. "Just something to keep in mind."

CHAPTER 13

I walked on the beach in the afternoon. The tide was coming in, so I had to do quick side steps every once in a while to avoid the occasional wave that encroached farther up on the sand and threatened to engulf my shoes. It reminded me of what the Buddhists say about everything being in a continual state of change. No matter how permanent something might appear to be, it is in the midst of a constant process of creation and destruction. None of us has a permanent self; we are just our thoughts, which are new every moment. Our memories are all we can claim as lasting, but even they are reinterpreted every time we recall them.

That frightened me because I knew my recollections over the last few years were all I had. Without them I'd go back to being the naïve college grad who had enlisted in the Army for no good reason. I didn't want those memories to change. However painful they might be, I clung to them like my favorite childhood teddy bear because they reminded me of a time when I had been part of something, something larger and more important than myself.

Later that evening I was sitting in my office at the yoga studio, watching as the students arrived for classes with Karen and Julie, now to be assisted by Charlie. When Charlie came in, he gave me a brief nod before heading into Julie's room. I thought he held his chin up an inch or so higher than before. Nothing like attention from a beautiful young woman to put a little strut in a man's step. I reminded myself that I still had to have a talk with Charlie about his past, and decided I'd catch him after class.

I had told Karen that Lauren was supposed to come see me before class, and asked Karen to remind her of this as soon as she showed up. When it was time to begin, Karen came out to my office and shook her head.

"No Lauren," she announced, her disappointment obvious.

I nodded.

"I guess she's too upset over Dr. Jim to come out."

"I told her to be here."

"Maybe you should be more gentle with her. She's still rather fragile."

"I'm going to go see her at home."

"We could both visit her after class is over," Karen suggested.

I could see by Karen's expression that she didn't think I had enough sensitivity for the job of talking to the recently bereaved. Maybe she was right. I wasn't going to argue the point with her.

"We'll see," I replied.

As soon as I heard Karen's class start, I checked my computer where I keep an updated list of the addresses and phone numbers for my current students, prepared for the day when I actually develop a mailing list. I called Lauren's number, but there was no answer. I figured she could be at home but might not want to explain why she had blown me off. I paused for a moment, considering Karen's offer to accompany me, then decided I didn't want interference from a gentle, caring heart. After all, I wasn't going there to comfort Lauren, but to get information. I glanced at the computer screen once more to memorize her address, then pulled out my official Cornwall Chamber of Commerce map and found its location. I grabbed my jacket and headed out the door. If I was lucky, I'd be back before class was over.

Lauren lived on Hazlett Road. When I got there, I found it was a relatively short street of maybe ten houses. It was near the beach and dead-ended into a small forest of pine trees. Lauren's house was the last but one from the end. It was a Cape Cod style with two dormer windows in the front and a single car attached garage on the side. There were no lights on that I could see, but I went up to the front door and rang the bell anyway. I waited but there was no answer. I opened the glass storm door and knocked on the off chance the bell wasn't working—still no response.

I stood there, feeling my anger build. I suspected she had anticipated that I might try to see her and had purposely gone out just to avoid talking to me. Muttering to myself that I'd never wanted to take the damned case in the first place, I walked around to the side of the house by the garage. There was a window into the garage. I peered inside, hoping to spot whether her car was still there. If it was, I intended to keep ringing the bell until I woke the dead.

I couldn't see much in the darkened garage, but I did hear something, the rumbling of a car engine. I rushed around to the front and tried to raise the garage door, but it wouldn't budge. The front door of the house was a solid piece of wood with a sturdy lock, so I went around to the back door, which had nine small panes of glass in the upper half. The door was locked, so I took off my jacket, wrapped it carefully around my arm and used my elbow to break out the pane nearest the door handle. Fortunately the deadbolt hadn't been set, and after some one-handed fumbling around, I managed to turn the inside knob and open the door.

I went into the kitchen and immediately smelled exhaust fumes. I spotted what had to be the door to the garage. When I pulled it open, a wave of carbon monoxide made me stagger back a step, but I forced myself to keep going. I found a light switch to my right. I turned on the lights and saw Lauren behind the wheel. There was an electric door opener on the wall to my left. I pushed the button and the motor started to lift the door. Immediately a gust of cool air began to blow away the fumes. I pulled open the car door. Lauren had the unnaturally rosy look of someone with carbon monoxide poisoning.

I dragged her out of the car, lifted her over my shoulder, and carried her down the driveway. I put her down as gently as I could on the lawn. After using my cell phone to call 911, I began giving her mouth-to-mouth. I didn't think it would help, but I kept it up until I heard the sirens coming up the street.

A half hour later I was leaning against my car in front of Lauren's house. The ambulance had already left, but Jack and a couple of patrolmen were still standing by the garage. I watched Jack walk down the driveway toward me.

"Are you all right?" he asked.

"Yeah," I said. He'd asked me the same question when he first arrived. I didn't think frequent updates were necessary. If he asked me again, I might really tell him the truth.

He stood next to me and we looked past the house next door and into the darkness of the woods.

"Do you think she did this because of losing Dr. Jim?" he asked.

I shrugged.

"She certainly waited long enough, if that was the reason," Jack continued.

"Not really. You hear about lots of cases of war vets who only develop post-traumatic stress years after they've come home. Sometimes loss is a corrosive. It takes a while to eat through to your center."

Jack glanced over at me but didn't say anything.

"You said that she was doing some investigating on her own?"

"Yeah. But she wouldn't tell me what she'd found out. I

came over here hoping to get it out of her. Now I wish I'd made it sooner."

"Probably wouldn't have mattered. This wasn't a cry for help. Lauren was serious and would have tried again and again until she got it right. She had both doors to the house locked, and there were no lights on. If you hadn't looked in the garage window, there's no telling when her body would have been found. She took a lot of trouble not to be stopped."

"Somebody took a lot of trouble."

He glanced at me again.

"What are you getting at?"

"Lauren sounded more disappointed than sad the last time I talked to her. Like I told you, she'd found something out about Dr. Jim that didn't fit with her picture of him. In fact she seemed angry about what he had done, and angry people don't usually kill themselves, at least not until after they've dealt with the person they're angry at."

Jack paused. "So are you suggesting that somebody murdered her?"

"I'd like you to keep in mind," I said. "I smelled alcohol on her breath when I was trying to resuscitate her."

"She may have had a few drinks to work up her courage."

"Or maybe somebody spiked her drink, so she'd be easy to carry out to the car."

"Well, there'll be an autopsy, of course, and the crime scene boys from the state police will give everything a once-over. Based on what you're telling me, I'll make sure it's a thorough one." Jack gave me a sad smile. "If you could come up with the name of a suspect, that would make things even easier."

"I'm afraid I haven't gotten that far yet."

"So you're going to keep investigating?"

"I guess I don't have much choice now. Lauren's death leaves it kind of open-ended for me. But I don't have any really good idea where to go next."

"If you come up with one, you'll let me know?" Jack asked.
"Sure," I said out loud. *Eventually*, I added to myself.

Chapter 14

I slept badly that night. I think it was because of what I'd said to Jack about Lauren not killing herself over a guy who had disappointed her. Even when I'd said it, it had sounded phony, a logical response that doesn't get at the reality of experience. I suspect I wanted it to be true more than I really thought it was. Anyway, I'm certain that's why I dreamed about the attack.

There was no good reason we happened to be going down that road in Iraq on that particular day. We were Military Police after all, and there was no compelling reason to leave base. There was certainly enough activity to keep us busy without going out to look for more.

I think it all began right after I'd asked the captain what he planned to do after leaving the military. He started getting restless. Before that, he would happily spend the afternoon sitting at his desk, carefully reading every report and occasionally calling one of our off-duty people into his office to explain why some barroom drunk had managed to get the drop on him when he was breaking up a brawl. Although, to be fair, he never reprimanded anyone without offering suggestions as to how the situation might be approached differently in the future.

But after our conversation, he began ignoring the paperwork, signing off on reports without reading them, and he was either unwilling or unable to focus on the many details involved in running an M.P. unit. His attitude toward me also changed. I sat outside his office handling all the lower-level decisions and making duty assignments. We'd always maintained strict military decorum, although I'd become accustomed to his suddenly smiling in the middle of giving me orders and suggesting we get together that night. Looking back, I think part of the thrill of our relationship was the mixture of the formal with the down and dirty. It all seemed like a very romantic adventure. It was, after all, a clandestine affair that could have gotten both of us in a lot of hot water.

But as the restlessness set in, he became more and more impatient, hurriedly telling me what to do then rushing off to do who knew what. Men began to complain that he would suddenly appear while they were out on patrol to check up on them. And more and more he began to take over investigations that should have been left to subordinates. More worrisome to me: he hardly ever suggested that we get together anymore. When I suggested it, he would say he was too busy, although I knew he spent most of his evenings alone in his quarters or else playing cards with other officers.

Then along came Private First Class Johnny Teague. I never actually met PFC Teague, but he was something of a legend around the unit. He'd gone AWOL almost immediately after the fall of Baghdad and had never been seen again. Although his file was still kept open, we pretty much assumed he had died in some alley, either the victim of the insurgency or of criminal elements he had taken up with in order to survive. But one bright, dry, windblown morning a report came over my computer showing that a Military Police unit in Baghdad had picked up PFC Teague in a sweep of local drug dealers.

I had rushed into the captain's office, told him of the arrest, and expressed my delight at the possibility of our finally apprehending this legendary AWOL. I conveyed my enthusiasm too well. The captain got a shrewd smile on his face, and his eyes sparkled.

"Let's arrange to go pick him up ourselves."

"There's no need for that, sir. The unit in Baghdad makes several runs a week up to the airport. They'll bring him along the next time they come up."

Baghdad was ten miles away. A fast fifteen-minute run, given the rate of speed most drivers wanted to maintain.

"We lost him. We should be the ones to bring him back."

"It's true he went AWOL from the infantry division we're attached to, but we usually let whoever picks them up return them to us."

"Not this time," he said in a tone that I knew meant he wouldn't listen to any further arguments.

"What do you want to do, sir?"

"There must be a convoy of some kind heading down to Baghdad. Get us in on it."

"When, sir?"

He glared at me as if the question were foolish, although I doubted any rush was necessary since Teague wouldn't be going anywhere.

"As soon as possible," he said with a sarcastic edge.

I turned and walked out of his office.

Shortly after dawn the next morning we pulled in at the end of a convoy heading down to Baghdad. I'd heard that the first convoy of the morning was always the most dangerous because the enemy had probably spent the night putting explosive charges along the sides of the road. But "as soon as possible" meant just that, and I wasn't about to go back to the captain with the suggestion that we be prudent and leave after noon.

The captain was driving, and I was riding shotgun carrying an M16. Up in the turret of our Humvee, manning the M240 Bravo machine gun, was Private Bobby Ames, whom everyone called Junior, probably because he was named after his father, although it could have been because of his appearance. He hardly looked to be seventeen. All I'd heard about him was that he came from the Midwest. As a virtual Bostonian, that was a part of the world I knew even less about than Iraq.

The rest of the convoy was made up of an armored personnel carrier in the lead, a deuce and a half truck, and two more Humvees ahead of ours. I didn't like being on the end, but then, I wouldn't have been much happier being anywhere else. I've never thought of myself as a coward, but I didn't see the point in taking unnecessary chances. But the captain was really into this. His voice was light and happy, and he joked around. He even called me "Ali" the way he had before our conversation about his possible retirement. I figured if this was going to bring things back to the way they were, then it was worth a little risk.

We'd been on the road about ten minutes, and the outlying suburbs of Baghdad were in sight when we got hit. Whoever set off the bomb—I heard afterwards that it was radio operated—made a decision that saved my life. The explosion went off right under the Humvee five yards in front of us, blowing it high in the air. The captain immediately stopped our vehicle. The cloud of dust and debris combined with the ear-shattering sound left all of us stunned for a moment. As soon as the dust settled, we saw that the Humvee had come down across the road, partially blocking our way forward. The captain maneuvered to get closer, stopping when the smoking vehicle was a couple of yards ahead of us on our right side.

"I'm going to check it out," he said, starting to open his door.

What sounded like pebbles began striking the sides of the vehicle, and he quickly pulled the door closed. I saw the window next to his head begin to pock with the marks of bullets. I heard the M240 Bravo kick in over my head and knew that Junior had sprung into action.

The captain reached over and gave me a hard shove.

"Let's move, Randall, we have to get out on your side."

I jerked the handle back. Just then there was a loud explosion above my head that rocked our vehicle forward until I thought it would roll over. I rolled out the door into a crouch and looked up. The turret that Junior had been in was gone, sheared off by a rocket-propelled grenade.

I knelt down by the right rear bumper.

"I'm going up front and see if there's anyone alive in the other vehicle," the captain said, putting his lips close to my ear but still having to shout over the sound of gunfire coming from our left. "Keep your head down and don't shoot unless you have a clear target."

I took a quick glance over my left shoulder at the field running alongside the road on our right. No heads had popped up there, thank God, or we'd be surrounded. I could hear the whine of bullets glancing off the far side of our Humvee. I didn't think the shooters could see anyone to aim at, but that apparently didn't discourage them from maintaining their fire. I glanced over my right shoulder and saw that the captain had the door from the other Humvee open and was pulling someone out.

As I turned my eyes back down the road behind us, I saw a figure run out into the middle of the highway. He crouched down right on the centerline and put a rocket launcher up to his shoulder. I raised my rifle. We fired at the same time. I never saw what happened to him because an instant later I was pitched forward on my face as the damaged Humvee just ahead of ours blew up.

I blacked out for a while. I'm not sure how long, but when I tried to scramble back to my feet, my left hip wouldn't move. I looked down and saw a dark stain spreading over my upper thigh. I reached up to touch what felt like water on my right cheek and my hand came away covered in blood. Deciding in a rush of panic that I couldn't stay where I was, I leaned against our vehicle and started to push myself up into a standing position. Inside me was a voice telling me to run somewhere, anywhere. That would probably have gotten me killed by gunfire from the field on the far side of the road. Fortunately, after taking two steps I collapsed. I leaned my back against the side of our vehicle with my legs splayed out in front of me—a position I knew must look weak and helpless. Not a posture I wanted to die in. I craned my neck, trying to see what had happened to the captain, but couldn't make out anything because the other Humvee had its door bent out in a way that blocked my view. I heard the sound of machine gun fire coming toward me from up the road. I felt a sweet rush of relief when I realized it must be the rest of our convoy returning to get us.

I rolled over on my hands and knees, sending a jolt of pain through my left hip that made me scream. I started to crawl forward slowly to see if I could find the captain. I must have fainted somewhere along the way because the next thing I remember, a sergeant was staring down at me and telling me to remain still.

"I have to find my captain," I said, trying to struggle to my knees. "I have to see him."

A firm hand held me in place while he injected me with something. "No," he said. "You don't want to see him."

I started to protest, struggling to regain my feet. But then there was a flash of intense pain and darkness came over me.

It wasn't until five days later that I regained some semblance of clear consciousness again. During that time I'd undergone surgery and been filled with enough painkillers to separate me completely from the combat hospital around me by a warm fuzzy blanket. By day five, I had come down enough that the staff thought I was ready to have a visit from my battalion's commanding officer. Since the battalion's headquarters was at a distant location on our sprawling base from where our company was stationed, I'd only seen him on a few occasions when he visited the captain.

He was whippet thin in a neatly creased uniform and looked to be in his late forties. He sat on the side of my bed instead of standing over me, a gesture that seemed incredibly caring to me at the time. It also prevented me from having to look up, which was a blessing since somewhere along the way I had also managed to give my neck a bad sprain.

We began by talking about my condition. He told me that I'd be evacuated home in the next couple of days and repeated what the doctors had already told me about my need for rehabilitation because of damage to the muscles in my hip. He smiled and said a few encouraging words about how a woman M.P. should have no trouble overcoming a minor obstacle like that. I'd smiled back, not believing a word but pleased to hear him say it anyway.

Then we got down to business as he asked me to explain why the captain and I had been in the convoy. There wasn't much I could say in justification of the captain's decision to head off the base toward Baghdad. The more I tried to emphasize the need to get custody of Johnny Teague, the more it sounded like an unnecessary lark by an officer bored at remaining on base. I was sure the major thought so as well, although he carefully refrained from seeming critical by either word or expression. And even though our little adventure had gotten the captain and Junior killed and put me out of action indefinitely, I knew enough about the Army by then to realize the report would be phrased so as to say nothing negative about a career officer with a record like the captain's.

When the major stood up next to my bed after our little chat, I noticed he had some buff-colored personnel folders in his hand. He opened one.

"Sergeant, you've requested that your family not be notified if you are injured unless that injury is life threatening." He gave me a small smile. "Since you are apparently going to live, are you sure you don't want me to notify your family of your condition?"

"I'd rather that you didn't, sir. We really aren't very close."

He nodded. "I'll follow your wishes."

"Sir, who will be making the arrangements for the captain?" I asked.

"He has a family."

"But I know that he was estranged from his children. And he was divorced from his wife. I'm not really sure he's got anyone at home to take care of things."

The major frowned and opened another folder.

"It says here that he was married."

"There must be some mistake."

The major held the folder open in front of my eyes and pointed to the checked box next to "married." The expression on my face must have told him something, or else there was a lot more base scuttlebutt about my relationship with the captain than I thought, because he put a hand on my shoulder.

"I don't know how the captain felt about his marriage, but you know the Army. We have to go by the rules. His wife will be in charge of making the arrangements." He patted my shoulder like a kindly uncle. "Put all of this behind you, Randall, and focus on getting well. The Army needs people like you."

It turned out the first of those was impossible and the second wasn't true, but I'm sure the major meant well. And if some well-intentioned orderly had come by at that moment and offered me an end-of-the-road cocktail, would I have taken it down in one big gulp, happy to find an easy way out of my disappointment? I'm not sure. So, the lesson was that even if Lauren was disappointed in Dr. Jim, she still might have considered him worth dying for, and I shouldn't be so quick to ignore the depths of her despair. But my doubts remained.

CHAPTER 15

I was later than usual getting to the yoga center the next morning because I had spent extra time doing Sun Salutations and working on the Hero pose. I also struggled with meditation as my mind kept wandering into dark places. I probably should have given up after the first five minutes, but I kept on doggedly for another twenty with little success. When meditation ends up making you more frustrated rather than less, you're probably missing the point.

I marched up the stairs as fast as my hip would allow and walked into the lobby to find Karen, Julie, and Charlie sitting there silently, as if at a wake. Karen glanced up and studied my face.

"Do you know about Lauren?" she asked.

I nodded. "I found her."

"Oh, you poor thing," Karen said, starting to get to her feet. I suspected a hug was in the offing and gave a sharp downward gesture with my hand, the kind you might give to an affectionate but annoying dog. Karen looked a bit hurt but resumed her seat.

"How did you find out?" I asked.

"The woman who owns the store where I buy my morning paper heard it from somebody," Karen replied.

"I see."

"So you decided to go out to see Lauren without me after all?" Karen asked.

I detected an accusatory tone, as if Lauren would be frolicking among the living if only I hadn't decided to pull a lone ranger.

"Yeah."

"I offered to go with you," she said.

"Under the circumstances, it's just as well you didn't."

"I didn't know Lauren all that well," Julie said. "Do they think it was suicide?"

"They won't know for sure until they get the medical examiner's report, but I guess it usually is in cases like this," I answered.

There was no way I was going to tip my hand that I thought Lauren's death might be murder. If I did, it would be all around Cornwall by tomorrow.

"Don't blame yourself. It wasn't your fault," Karen said unconvincingly.

"Why should Ali blame herself?" Julie asked.

I guessed that for once curiosity had won out over Julie's desire to stay ignorant and uninvolved in the problems of others. Or else her relationship with Charlie was bringing her out of her shell.

I turned to Julie and Charlie, who were sitting together on the same bench.

"Lauren asked me to look into the disappearance of her fiancé."

"That doctor who disappeared off of Turtle Island," Karen added.

"Did you find out anything?" a hoarse voice asked.

It took me a second to realize that Charlie had made a contribution to the conversation. When I looked at him in surprise, his eyes immediately returned to studying the carpet.

"Not very much," I answered.

"Why would you blame yourself for her death?" he continued, still not looking up.

"I didn't say I did."

I stared at Karen, who fidgeted nervously on her bench.

"Well, people sometimes do feel guilty even when it isn't rational," Karen replied, speaking to Charlie as if she were a teacher and he a slightly slow student.

He shook his head. "That's stupid. We all have enough things we've actually done to feel guilty about. There's no reason to feel guilty about stuff that isn't our fault."

I reminded myself that I really had to find out more about Charlie's background.

"I was only trying to help by telling you not to blame yourself," Karen said to me with a pleading expression.

"I know you were," I said sincerely. Even though Charlie had spoken with the voice of wisdom, I had to admit Karen had come closer to the truth. I felt guilty as hell because I hadn't come up with the right answers to save Lauren's life.

I made a show of looking at the Buddha clock on the table next to Karen.

"Well, the students will be here any minute, so I guess we had better go into the practice rooms and start getting ready. We may have other things on our minds, but we have to center ourselves and be prepared to teach."

That was a completely unnecessary pep talk, but it gave me an excuse to nod briskly to the troops and make an escape into my office.

I spent the next hour trying to organize a mailing list on my computer. I thought I just about had it done when the phone rang. It was Dianne Schianno.

"I don't know what it's all about," she began then paused. "So I decided to call you."

"What are you talking about?" I asked.

"The police returned Jim's car to me. Since we're still married, I guess they figured that it belonged here."

142

"Yeah. No point leaving it parked by his empty apartment. That's just an invitation to a thief."

"When . . . if he comes back, I guess it might as well be here waiting for him," she said.

"And the car is important in some way?"

"Right, well indirectly. Jim's light fall jacket was in the back of the car. I was kind of surprised that the police left it there."

"They probably checked the pockets. But since there hasn't actually been a crime, I guess they saw no point in keeping it as evidence."

"Well, the lining of the pocket was ripped. And there was a note that had slipped down inside behind the lining."

"What did the note say?"

"It tells Jim to be at the Turtle Island Beach by eight o'clock and to have the money with him. It also warns him not to tell anyone else and not to be late."

"Will you be home for the next half hour?"

"Yes."

"I'll be right over."

When I arrived at the Schiannos', Dianne met me at the door and took me down the hall to the kitchen. It was large and airy. It had probably been cutting edge twenty years ago. I wasn't surprised. Neither of the Schiannos struck me as very materialistic, and they did have to worry about college for their two boys.

"Would you like some coffee?" she asked.

I turned it down, not mentioning that with my sleeping problem, chamomile was probably too strong. She went over to the counter, picked up a half sheet of paper, and held it out to me. The note had been written on a computer. I asked her to put it down on the counter again. There was no sense in adding my fingerprints to those already there.

The well-creased note, which had obviously been folded up

several times by either the sender or Dr. Jim, said pretty much what she had already told me. The writer told Jim to be at the end of Monroe Street by the beach at eight o'clock, to bring the money, and not to tell anyone where he was going. The only additional point I noticed was that the top of the note, as a greeting, said, "Dr. Schianno." That indicated to me that the person who sent the note was probably not a patient. A patient would have known that he went by Dr. Jim. I wondered why there was any need to put his name on it at all if it had been addressed to him, unless the person for some reason wanted to remind Jim that he was a doctor.

"Did you find the envelope?" I asked.

Dianne shook her head. "I was lucky to find this. When I picked up the jacket, I just happened to grab it where the letter was in the lining. I felt something stiff and hunted around for it."

"So Jim probably shoved the letter in his pocket and it slipped through. I assume he didn't mention anything to you about being blackmailed."

"Do you think that's what this is all about?"

"What do you think?"

"Well, it could be that he was helping some woman and arranged to meet her and give her some money. After all, that's the kind of thing he did."

"The tone of the note sounds awfully demanding for someone requesting help. Plus you doubted that Jim would give some woman ten thousand out of your joint bank account."

"I didn't think so. Although now I'm starting to wonder whether I ever knew Jim at all."

The similarity of her comment to the one Lauren had made shortly before she died made me pause. Jim the chameleon, I thought. All his women thought they knew him, and apparently none of them really did.

"So you don't have any clue what this note could have been about."

Dianne shook her head.

"Aside from his acting strangely for the week or so before he disappeared, you have no idea if he was in any kind of trouble."

"No."

I nodded. "Did you know that Lauren died last night?"

I hadn't intended to shock her. I figured she probably knew. Ever since I was a kid, people have told me I'm not real sensitive when it comes to the feelings of others; that I tend to say what I mean without a lot of soothing embellishments. The truth may make you free, but I've discovered it doesn't make you a lot of friends. I've worked on changing my approach, but this time I forgot. I could tell, because Dianne turned pale and gripped the edge of the counter. She staggered a few steps and sat down hard on one of the bar stools where the kids probably ate breakfast.

"Lauren's dead? How?"

"Carbon monoxide poisoning in her garage."

"Oh, God. So it was suicide, then?"

"Apparently," I said, once again keeping any trace of skepticism out of my voice.

Dianne ran a hand through her hair. "I feel so bad. I always thought Lauren was this shallow little girl with a daddy complex who somehow managed to catch Jim at a vulnerable moment in his life."

I shrugged. "Even shallow girls can get upset and turn the ignition key."

"But don't you think it shows she cared deeply for him?"

"I'm sure she needed him. That's something different."

Dianne gave me a puzzled look. "Why are you so reluctant to say she loved him? I'm his wife and I can face it. Why can't you?"

"I'm not sure what love is, but I'm pretty sure that a good percentage of what passes for it isn't the real thing."

"What is it, then?" she asked with a trace of defiance in her voice.

"Obsession, habit, dependency, a desire for domination— who knows? But they're the more common human emotions. Love is actually pretty rare."

She thought about what I'd said for a moment.

"Maybe you're right. It wasn't very long after we moved here before I realized Jim and I didn't have very much in common. Oh, we got along okay, but sometimes I would think that love had to be more than this. But by then we were married, and how could I divorce a man who had saved my life, at least figuratively, and maybe literally? Would you say I stayed with him out of gratitude rather than love?"

Dianne stared at me as if my answer would actually make a difference in her life.

"I don't know," I said, avoiding the responsibility. "I'm sure love can be mixed in with a lot of other emotions."

She gave me a disappointed look, as if she guessed I was humoring her.

"But why did Lauren commit suicide now?" she asked.

"What do you mean?" I asked, even though I'd been asking myself the same question.

"It's been a week since Jim disappeared. I would have thought that she'd have been most distraught right after he went missing." She stopped and answered her own question. "Of course, the more time went by, the more she probably felt he was never coming back. It probably just wore her down. She never struck me as being very strong emotionally."

"She discovered something," I said.

"What do you mean?"

"The last time I talked to her, she indicated she had found

146

out something about Jim that shocked her."

"Shocked her in what way?"

"I don't know. But it was something he'd done that was completely out of character, and it seemed to upset her."

"I find that hard to believe," Dianne said, quickly leaping to her almost-ex-husband's defense and forgetting her earlier comment that she didn't really know him.

"So did Lauren."

My words rocked her back a bit. She bit her lip for a moment, then asked, "So you think Jim might actually have been involved in something that was so bad, it drove Lauren over the edge?"

"It's possible."

"That would mean Jim probably won't be coming back. If he did something so bad, then he'll keep running. Do you have any idea what it could have been?"

"No, but somebody does," I said, nodding in the direction of the note. "Or at least did."

"Why did you use the past tense?"

"Blackmail is a risky business. The person being blackmailed can feel cornered and desperate."

"You think Jim killed the person who wrote this note to keep him or her quiet?"

"Possibly."

"But then why run away?" Dianne asked.

"I don't know. Unless he thought the murder could be traced to him."

"Do you think Lauren found out Jim was a murderer?"

I shrugged. "I have no idea. She didn't live long enough to tell me."

The woman sighed and looked across the kitchen and out the window to the pleasant back yard as if she hoped to see something that would bring her back to her old life.

"What are you going to do next?"

"Why should I do anything next? I was acting for Lauren, and now that she's gone nobody is going to gain much if I pursue matters further."

Dianne gave me a knowing smile. "I don't think you're the kind of person who gives up so easily. Especially when the person you promised to help has taken her own life. You still feel obligated to find out what happened to Jim, don't you?"

Her confidence that she knew my mind annoyed me, especially since she was right.

"Feeling an obligation and being able to carry it out are two different things," I responded. "I have no idea what Lauren found out about your husband, and I'm not sure how to begin tracing Lauren's steps."

"I'm sure you'll think of something." She clearly had greater faith in my abilities than I did.

I picked the note up with a napkin and slipped it into a plastic sandwich bag Dianne provided. I'd drop it off at the police station on the way home. I didn't have much hope of finding useful fingerprints, but sometimes you get surprised. Dianne walked me to the front door. Then she kept going, and we strolled down the walk and out to the driveway together. I glanced back toward the garage and saw a Chevrolet sedan parked off to the side.

"Is that Jim's car?"

Dianne nodded.

"Maybe I should take a look through it. Probably the police have already found everything I would, but it pays to be thorough."

Dianne nodded and went into the house for the keys. I walked up the drive and examined the outside of the car, recalling that I had seen a bill for auto body repairs among Dr. Jim's bills.

"The garage did a good job. You'd never know it had been

damaged," I commented to Dianne when she returned.

She gave me a puzzled look.

"Jack and I went through your husband's bills. There was one for auto body repairs."

"From how long ago?"

I paused to think. "June. About three months ago."

"That's odd. Jim bought this car about then. I was kind of surprised when he bought it."

"Why's that?" I asked over my shoulder. I'd taken the keys and opened the back door. I was down on my knees and tilted to one side to keep the stress off my hip, as I checked under the front seat.

"He loved the BMW he had. It wasn't new, but he thought it was classy."

"A BMW does sound more like a doctor's car," I said, sliding further into the car to check under the passenger side.

"That's kind of what he said when I asked him why he'd changed. He said he was tired of being the stereotypical doctor with the fancy car. Then he'd laughed and said, particularly because he didn't have the income to go with it."

"If it was the BMW he had into the shop, it couldn't have been damaged much. The bill was only two hundred dollars."

"I didn't know it had been damaged at all."

"You hadn't seen anything wrong with it?"

She smiled. "I didn't come running out to examine the car every time Jim visited."

"Would the boys have noticed?"

She thought about my question. "If they were around and certainly if they went anywhere with their father, they'd have noticed. They're at an age when they're starting to be interested in cars."

"And would they have told you?"

"Hard to know. They're also at an age where they don't tell

their mother everything. They certainly wouldn't tell me if their father asked them not to."

I shifted to the front seat and checked the glove box, then searched around for all the obscure little storage areas car companies seem to believe are wanted by consumers. When I was done, I popped the trunk and the hood, and climbed out of the car.

"So your husband might not have told you if he'd been in an accident?" I asked, lifting up the hood. I poked around, just in case Jim had hidden something in the vicinity of the engine. I slammed the hood down, and looked at Dianne for an answer.

"He was proud of his driving, and if he'd gotten into an accident he thought was his own fault, he wouldn't mention it."

I went around to the back of the car and opened the trunk.

Jim was either neat or had transferred what mattered to a new escape car. There was nothing in the trunk. I lifted up the floor mat and checked around the jack and emergency spare with no better luck.

"But if it was the BMW that was damaged, why would Jim get his car repaired and then sell it immediately afterwards?" she asked.

The same question had been going through my mind.

"The insurance might cover the cost of repairs, and he'd get a lot more money for it on resale. On the other hand, his insurance premiums would go up. His answer to you about why he'd shift from a BMW to a Chevy sounds a little weak."

"I wasn't completely convinced myself at the time. I thought maybe he'd given the BMW to Lauren or sold it to get money to buy her something. I was angry and jealous, but I didn't want to make an issue of it."

I closed the trunk and turned to face her.

Dianne nodded. "Will the news of Lauren's death be a major newspaper story?"

"I imagine it will be, at least regionally. Why?"

"Maybe if Jim reads about it, he'll come back. If he realizes a woman committed suicide because of him, I think his conscience would force him to come back home."

I nodded and thanked her for her help. As I walked down the driveway, I figured maybe the Jim everyone thought they knew would come running home when he heard the news of Lauren's death, but I wasn't sure the real Jim would be so quick to return.

CHAPTER 16

I stopped by the police station and dropped off the letter I'd gotten from Dianne. The sergeant behind the desk told me Jack wasn't there. He reluctantly took the bag from me, staring at the contents as if it might be a letter bomb.

"It's a blackmail note," I said.

His expression changed from suspicious to incredulous. Now, maybe my appearance doesn't inspire confidence in elderly ladies or provoke spontaneous outpourings of affection from small children. But this guy should have been made of sterner stuff. However, he was clearly so put off by my punk hair, scarecrow figure, and piercing eyes that I was afraid he'd already dismissed me as a crank and would throw the bag away as soon as I left the office.

"The lieutenant will want to see the note," I said.

"Sure," he said in a dismissive tone that annoyed me even more. A familiar red curtain began descending over my mind. I forced it back up. Attacking a police office right in the station house would be too much for even Jack to overlook.

"I guess I couldn't take a look at the evidence the lieutenant and I brought back from Jim Schianno's place."

"Of course not," he said without a moment's hesitation, clearly surprised that Jack and I would have done anything together.

"How about giving the lieutenant a call and finding out?"

His blue eyes grew hard. "I'm busy."

"Aren't we all? Couldn't you spare just one minute to make the call?" I asked in a wheedling tone, trying to seem feminine and vulnerable. I figured that might work with him. It didn't. A mixture of fear and loathing came over his face, as if he'd suddenly seen a man turn into a woman.

"I'll tell him you were here," he muttered, stepping back.

I pressed both hands on the counter and leaned forward. Something in my face must have made him nervous. He took a further step back and his right hand came closer to his gun.

"Tell him now," I said. "The lieutenant and I are working on this investigation together. He won't be happy when he finds out you're slowing things down."

I could see him struggling between playing it safe careerwise and not giving an inch to a crazy woman.

I'm not sure how this would have eventually played out, because at that moment Jack came walking down the back hall from the parking lot.

"Hi, Alison," he called out. "Can I help you?"

"As I was just explaining to your desk sergeant here, I'd like to take a look at Dr. Jim's checkbook."

There was tension in my voice, and the red curtain was still hovering at the edge of my vision. I pushed it back hard. I didn't want to embarrass myself in front of Jack.

Jack's eyes went from my face to the sergeant's as he detected that a volatile situation needed to be defused.

"I'll get it for you," he said softly. He turned to the sergeant. "Thanks, Mike. I'll take care of this."

When he came back, I told him that I had just delivered a blackmail letter. The sergeant made a beeline over to his desk and brought it to Jack like a faithful retriever.

I went through the list of cancelled checks and jotted down the information I wanted. When I was done, I looked up to find Jack reading the letter through the plastic bag.

"Any idea what this was all about?" he asked.

I shook my head. "Dianne claims to know nothing about it. But Dr. Jim took a large chunk of change out of their joint account shortly after he received it, and I'm betting the money ended up on the beach with him that night."

Jack nodded his head. He slid the checkbook across the counter and turned it toward himself.

"What were you looking at?"

I showed him the slip of paper where I'd written down the name of the garage. "I wanted to check out the auto body shop where I believe Jim had some work done on his BMW."

"What's so strange about getting body work done?"

"Just that he sold the car immediately afterwards and bought a Chevy."

Jack smiled. "You don't think anyone would ever replace a piece of German engineering with an American product. Where's your patriotism?"

"I've never known a BMW owner who wasn't a bit of a car snob. So, no, I don't see him making the switch, especially after paying for body work."

"What's the name of the shop?"

"Carmody's."

Jack took the piece of paper and walked over to the desk where the sergeant was sitting. He made a small gesture and the sergeant scrambled out of the chair. Jack settled behind the computer and after a few sets of keystrokes, he wrote something down on the paper. Then he walked over to the counter and placed it in front of me. It gave the address and phone number of Carmody's Body Shop.

"Let me know what you find out."

"You don't want to be the one to check on it?"

He shrugged. "I've got meetings all day, and we're short-handed."

"Most police departments would want to keep a civilian from getting involved."

Jack shrugged. "You wouldn't stay on the sidelines even if I asked you to. At least this way I get to know what you've discovered."

I didn't say anything to that.

"Plus I know that you need to find out what happened. It matters to you, especially now that Lauren's dead."

I automatically started to say that nothing involving other people mattered very much to me. But I stopped, because I realized it wasn't true. Lauren had asked me to help her and I had blown it, whether through some fault of my own or not. And now I wanted—no, more than that—I needed to find out what had happened to both Jim and Lauren.

"I'll let you know what I come up with," I promised.

"If you need any official juice, refer them to me."

I nodded, then I glared over Jack's shoulder at the sergeant who was seated again behind his desk, staring at the computer screen while trying to pick up what we were saying.

"He was only doing his job," Jack said softly.

I shook my head. "He was only doing his job in a stupid, officious manner that reminded me of all the times I've run into the same thing in the Army. Spare me from small men with a little power."

Jack lowered his voice even more. "I inherited him from the previous chief. His uncle's on the town council."

"You should keep an eye on him, because some day he'll screw things up for you big time."

Jack smiled. "Why do you think I've got him sitting behind a desk?"

Carmody's Body Shop was a good half-hour north of Cornwall in Scarborough, just south of Portland. Some days I might have taken Route 1 north and followed the scenic route as part of my practice of Tathatā, a Buddhist idea that emphasizes focusing on each moment as a unique combination of circumstances that has never occurred before and will never happen again. But today I just wanted to get on with it, so I hopped on Interstate 95.

As I headed north I wondered why Dr. Jim had chosen a body shop so far away from Cornwall to repair his BMW. Somewhere on the stretch from Kittery up to Kennebunk, there surely must be a body shop that could have done a competent job on his precious car, especially if he planned to resell it right away. Most people would have gone with the cheapest local place and hoped the future owner wouldn't look too closely.

Carmody's turned out to be located in a small industrial park a few miles outside of the downtown area. I drove around curving roads that went past neatly landscaped office buildings and light factories before I spotted the body shop.

Half-expecting to find ruined hulks of wrecked automobiles littering the yard and bringing down the neighborhood, I was surprised to see a neat garage with a facade done in some kind of brickface. Only the large doors indicated it was a garage at all, and I guessed all the vehicles awaiting service were carefully hidden behind the high fence encompassing the rear yard.

I walked in a regular-sized door marked "office" and was greeted by a middle-aged man with "Dave" sewn above his left pocket. He stood behind a long counter and seemed happy to see me.

"How can I help you?"

"I'm looking into a repair job you did for a Dr. Jim Schianno back in May."

A puzzled expression came over his face. "Looking into?"

"I'm helping the police down in Cornwall. The doctor has disappeared, so we're trying to follow up on his activities for the last few months before he left town."

I could see him wondering if he should demand to see some credentials before sharing the information. But then he gave a mental shrug and turned to the computer and tapped several keys. This was repeated a number of times. Finally he stopped with a surprised expression on his face.

"You'll have to talk to the boss about this," he said.

"Would that be Mr. Carmody?"

"Yeah. Roger Carmody."

We stood there looking at each other for a moment. I decided Dave was hoping I'd just walk out the door without asking any more questions.

"And would Mr. Carmody be available?" I finally asked, breaking the stalemate.

"I don't know. I'll check." Dave went down to the end of the counter and disappeared through a door into the back. He returned a few minutes later and motioned for me to follow him.

I went through the door, which gave me a glimpse of a garage bay divided off into separate spaces by large sheets of heavy plastic. Most of them seemed to have cars in them, and I saw a worker wearing a respirator about to start up a paint sprayer. The dull roar of a powerful ventilation system provided a steady, humming background tune. Dave led me up a flight of stairs into a nicely done office suite that contrasted with the humble work area downstairs. He ushered me into the first office, then slipped out quickly. A middle-aged woman sitting at a computer screen gave me an appraising glance. I don't think she immediately found me wanting, but she was certainly reserving judgment. I figured that was the best I could reasonably expect.

"Mr. Carmody will see you. Just go right down the hall and into the office at the end."

I went down the short hall into the office. It was a large, square room with very little furniture, but it had been painted a soothing color and had window curtains and shades that gave it a homey feel. The center of the room held a large desk that looked to be made out of an expensive wood. A fancy leather blotter occupied the surface and a folder was open in the center of it. One pen and a pair of reading glasses were next to the papers. The only other item on the desk was a vase of fresh flowers. I didn't think the short man with a barrel chest, who stood up from behind the desk when I entered, had put them there himself. I wondered whether the woman in the outer office was responsible, and whether she was more than a secretary, maybe even Mrs. Carmody. The man didn't offer to shake hands, but he did point to one of the nice pair of leather chairs right in front of the desk.

He had a full face with a lot of interesting wrinkles and the strong blunt fingers of a man used to doing things with his hands. I figured Mr. Carmody had started downstairs and worked his way up. He gave me a bland look as if unsure how much he wanted to tell me.

"You wanted to know about the work that we did several months ago for Dr. Schianno."

"That's right."

"Why do you want to know about the job I did for the doc?"

"As I told Dave, the doctor has disappeared, and I'm helping the police by looking into any unusual events that happened to Dr. Schianno in the last few months."

"Like getting his car damaged."

I nodded. "It doesn't happen every day."

"It does to someone." Carmody smiled, "And that's fortunate for me."

I returned his smile, and we sat looking at each other for a long moment.

"I didn't realize I'd have to see the owner to find out about a simple repair job," I finally said, making an effort to break the conversational roadblock. "Is auto body work always so confidential?"

"Dave brought you up here because the computer showed the job had been done for a much reduced price at my request."

"Yeah, I know he only paid two hundred. I figured you couldn't get a ding hammered out of a BMW for that price. The doc was a lucky man. Why was that?"

Carmody furrowed his brow, then nodded as if to himself. I figured he'd finally made a decision.

"A couple of years ago, I was having trouble with my breathing. I'd suddenly start wheezing and couldn't catch my breath, and almost fainted a couple of times. My local quack claimed I had an allergy. He said maybe I was developing asthma or something due to all the exposure to paint fumes over the years. I went to some guy who ran a lot of tests, but he didn't really come up with anything. Just gave me an inhaler that didn't do a damned bit of good."

I nodded sympathetically. I'd lived through my share of medical runarounds.

"So I was down in Cornwall on business, and I got one of these attacks. The worst one yet. It was so bad that the guy I was meeting with rushed me in to Dr. Jim's clinic. He almost had to carry me in from the car. I'm sure he would have taken me right to the emergency room, but I kept telling him that I wasn't going into any hospital because I knew I'd never come out." He smiled sheepishly. "Just a little phobia I have."

"Lots of people feel that way. So what did Dr. Jim tell you?"

"He knew right away it wasn't my damned lungs that were the problem, it was my heart. The old pump wasn't getting enough oxygen to my brain because of a leaky valve. He got me right in to see a cardiologist. I did end up having to go into the hospital to have surgery and get the valve replaced. But now

I'm fine." He tapped lightly on the center of his large chest to confirm the point.

"And you owed it all to Dr. Jim."

Carmody nodded. "I'd probably be dead today if it weren't for him. I told the doc that if he ever needed auto body work done to come see me and I'd be happy to do it for free."

"I'm sure patients say things like that to their doctors all the time. Were you a little surprised when he took you up on it?"

The man shrugged. "Maybe a little. Dr. Jim didn't strike me as a guy who was out for himself. But then I figured that he didn't come to me so much because he could get the job done for free—and anyway, he insisted on paying something—I finally decided he just wanted to make sure his BMW got the best treatment. He really loved that car."

"He sold it a few weeks later."

Carmody's eyebrows went up in surprise.

"He bought a Chevy," I added.

"Go figure," he said. "But you know with some guys once a car is damaged, no matter how well the vehicle's been repaired, it never looks quite right to them. Over time it really starts to bug them, and eventually they just have to get rid of it."

"Like somebody lying to you. You never feel quite the same about them again."

"Yeah, I guess," he said doubtfully.

"What was the damage you repaired?"

He stared into space and dramatically furrowed his brow.

"Right front bumper and fender," he finally said.

"Do you remember off the top of your head all the repairs that you've done?"

He laughed. It was a deep, rumbling sound.

"I took a personal interest in that one. Do you have any idea what it costs to replace a BMW bumper and fender?"

I shook my head.

"A lot. And I ate most of the cost. That's why I remember it. But, hey, it was worth it, considering what the doc did for me."

"Has anyone else been around asking about Dr. Jim's auto repair?"

Carmody wiggled himself further down in his big leather desk chair, then shook his head.

"Who else would come around asking?" he asked in a challenging tone.

"How about a woman named Lauren Malcolm?"

He shook his head. "Never heard of her. Who's she?"

"Dr. Jim's girlfriend."

"I didn't see her. And I'm sure that Dave or any of the other guys who work the desk downstairs would have brought her to me if she came by with a question, just like they did with you. Course I've been away for the past few weeks. But somebody would have told me about it."

"A vacation?"

He glanced down the hall. "Yeah, a special one. My wife and I went to Hawaii for our twenty-fifth anniversary."

"Congratulations," I said, standing up.

Carmody stood as well, and this time he shook hands with me.

"I'll be in touch if I have any more questions."

He nodded "Fine. But I've told you everything I know."

His eyes quickly slid away from mine, making me wonder what he'd left out.

CHAPTER 17

As I drove back from the auto body shop, I reviewed what I had learned. Dr. Jim had taken his car a good thirty miles outside of Cornwall to have it repaired. Now maybe he had done so because he expected Carmody to give him a deal. Some guys would naturally think that way. For them life is a complex web of personal favors and obligations they keep track of with great exactitude in their heads. They would expect to be able to cash in on what was owed to them, just as they would be willing to return a favor. But even Carmody had admitted he hadn't seen Dr. Jim as being that kind of a guy, and from what I'd learned about the doctor, neither did I. I could only think of one other reason he might have chosen a garage so far away from Cornwall. I decided to stop at the local library to confirm my suspicion.

I'd been told that the Cornwall Library was the result of a building boomlet that hit the town in the mid-seventies. The colonial house that had served for many years as the ornate and fully adequate home for all the books needed in the town was suddenly determined to be too small for a growing community. Benefitting from a state grant, the town fathers put up a simple brick building with colonial trim and a good-sized parking lot right along Route 1 where it would be convenient to the expanding population. It was convenient, one had to give them that. Unfortunately, today the style screamed institutional seventies and somehow managed to look more outdated than buildings in town that were a hundred years older.

Along with a new building, they had also hired a full-time library staff. So when I went up to the main desk, the woman was easily able to grant my request for the local daily newspapers going back two weeks before Dr. Jim brought his car into the garage. I figured the kind of story I'd be looking for would be on the front page, so I quickly scanned the headlines for those weeks. My search was rewarded by a story about an event that occurred the day before Jim brought his car into the garage.

An eight-year-old, named Eddie Wolfe had been hit by a car while playing outside his house on Hazlett Terrace, the same street Lauren had lived on. The boy resided with his grandmother. The newspaper carefully avoided assigning blame, but by reading between the lines, you could figure out that she might not have been the most attentive of caregivers. She hadn't been aware that Eddie was riding his bike out in the street at nine o'clock, well after it had gotten dark. She had been sitting in the living room, probably dozing in front of the television, when the squeal of brakes and the crunch of metal startled her. It may have taken her several moments to register what she had heard and feel concern. When she pulled open the front door, it was just in time to see a dark colored car racing off down the street and find her grandson dying in the middle of the road.

I checked the day of the week. The accident had happened on a Thursday, and I recalled Lauren telling me that Dr. Jim had always visited her on Thursdays. I leaned back and closed my eyes, letting the sunshine streaming through the window warm my face. What if Dr. Jim had been racing down Hazlett Terrace that night, his mind on all the problems in his complex life? A boy, possibly in dark clothes and riding his bike on a stretch of road that might have been poorly lighted, suddenly rolls out in front of him. There's the shock of impact. Maybe

Jim's immediate reaction is to stop and help the boy. He gets out of his car. A light comes on by the front door, so he knows someone will immediately call an ambulance. His professional and personal reputation being on the line, he gets back in the car and speeds away.

By the next day, he probably realizes that by leaving the scene of a fatal accident, he has made his situation much worse. So Jim decides that he has to hide his involvement at all costs. He takes his car to an auto body shop outside of the area, and on the off chance that someone at the accident scene was able to recognize the make, quickly gets rid of the car after it has been repaired, trading it in to buy the Chevy and get new plates. I hadn't remembered to check the dealer's name on the Chevy, but I was willing to bet that it was from a dealership far away from Cornwall.

So far the story sounded plausible. However, several things bothered me. The first was Lauren. Surely she was aware that the accident had occurred on her own street on the night Dr. Jim was to visit. Wouldn't she have asked Dr. Jim about it? Of course, she looked up to him so much that if he had denied any knowledge of the accident, she would probably have accepted his words without question. But wouldn't she have wondered when the car he was driving was suddenly replaced? Maybe he gave her some story about his wife insisting on having the BMW as part of their separation settlement. Everyone had attested to the fact that Jim was good at manipulating people for their own good. There was no reason to believe he wouldn't be just as skilled when it came to his own self-interest.

A more difficult question was: who had sent Dr. Jim the blackmail note? Someone must have seen the doctor racing away from the accident and gotten enough information to blackmail him. And who would resort to blackmail rather than report what he or she knew to the authorities?

Leaving that question aside as unanswerable without more information, I moved on to what might have happened the night Dr. Jim went to the beach. The most likely scenario was that he paid off his blackmailer. But perhaps something the blackmailer had said made the doctor realize the blackmail would never stop. So he decided to leave the area, choosing to start a new life where his crime would never be known. Given Jim's past skills at starting over, this scenario seemed like a real possibility. But would he have done it that very night, right after meeting with the blackmailer? You'd have thought he'd need a little lead time to plan things out.

A less likely alternative was that Jim had reached the conclusion about the unending nature of the blackmail and decided to kill his blackmailer, then leave town. I considered this idea less likely because Dr. Jim didn't strike me as a cold-blooded killer, and if you kill your blackmailer, why disappear and draw attention to yourself? More significantly, no one had been reported missing from the area other than Jim himself. And since it was likely the blackmailer would be a local, his or her disappearance would have been noticed.

The final question that bothered me was: who had killed Lauren? It seemed to me as though, when Lauren had expressed her disillusion with Dr. Jim shortly before her death, it was because she had begun to suspect him of being involved in Eddie Wolfe's death. That meant she had been doing some investigating on her own. Her poking around could have aroused the concern of two people: Dr. Jim and the blackmailer. Could Jim have somehow discovered that Lauren had unearthed his secret, and decided to kill her? Or could the blackmailer, afraid of having his blackmail plot revealed to the police, have decided to eliminate her? Dr. Jim wasn't a likely killer, but he might be desperate. The blackmailer was an unknown quantity.

I realized all this theorizing went far beyond the evidence

available to me, and I was in danger of turning the whole thing into a hopelessly complicated puzzle. I also became aware of having a raging headache, the kind that begins with a stiffening in the back of my neck, then surges through my jaw line and up into my head, another periodic reminder of my vacation in Iraq. Not as disabling as I'd heard migraines can be, they usually came on when I hadn't eaten and was under stress. My watch showed me it was already three o'clock, and I still hadn't found time for lunch. I returned the papers to the circulation desk and headed home.

CHAPTER 18

By the time I'd had a light lunch, it was too late for my usual walk on the beach. Clouds had moved in too, bringing with them a chilly breeze. I decided to nurse my headache by sitting in my loose version of a cross-legged position—the most I could master, given my hip—and consciously try to relax my neck and jaw. As much as I made the effort to keep focused on my breathing, my mind kept returning to the case, like a dog gnawing at a meatless bone. Every time it did, I gently pulled it back to my breath, which I consciously took in on a long inhale and let out with an even longer exhale.

Slowly my mind began to focus on the rhythm, and I felt relaxing energy begin to work its way up my spinal column. I lost track of time and was surprised when I finally opened my eyes and checked the clock to find I had been meditating for almost an hour. I was also pleased to discover that my headache had disappeared. Stretching my legs and massaging some feeling back into my bad hip, I awkwardly struggled to my feet with the help of a nearby chair.

I spent the next few hours catching up on my reading. I try to stay abreast of new trends in yoga and meditation, so I subscribe to several magazines in those fields. Usually I put them aside when they arrive, promising myself that some day when I am less busy or less stressed, I'll get around to reading them. Being the way I am, this often means several months of magazines are waiting for me when I do arrive at the day when the planets are in the proper alignment. When I finally finished the last magazine, I sat back and luxuriated in the feeling of virtue I was experiencing. Life was orderly again, so I could press onward.

Never a principled vegetarian, even during my time at the yoga center when it was strictly enforced, I usually avoided meat for health reasons, but would occasionally go off the wagon when I felt the need. Tonight I pulled a burger out of the freezer and quickly defrosted it in the microwave. I dumped some charcoal briquettes in the hibachi I kept on my deck and fired them up. Forty minutes later I was eating a nice juicy burger with some baked beans and a salad. As I slowly chewed, I thought about what I might do for the rest of the evening.

I was concerned that since I had missed my normal walk on the beach, I might find sleep elusive. The prospect of sitting up for hours, waiting for thoughts to leave my mind exhausted enough to lapse into unconsciousness, was a familiar but unpleasant one. I decided that attending Julie and Charlie's class might be a good way of using up some of my energy. It would also give me the appearance of being a real manager. After all, Charlie was a new teacher, so I should observe him teaching a class at least once before finally deciding whether or not to keep him on board. Plus, I still felt a certain responsibility to find out more about his past. Ananda had sent him to me for a reason, and I was sure there was more to his doing so than the fact that Charlie was an accomplished yoga practitioner.

I arrived at class shortly before it was due to begin at seven o'clock. There were about twelve people in the studio, a pretty good crowd. I attributed most of them to Julie's popularity, since a large part of the class was composed of the young and the beautiful. I noticed a couple of the women talking to Charlie, who was answering in a shy way with a lot of glances at the floor and small smiles. Rather than putting them off, the women seemed to find this rather charming. I had to admit such unassuming boyishness was kind of appealing, and I guessed this would be especially true for attractive young women who might have been aggressively hit on too often in their lives by men with exaggerated opinions of themselves. But Charlie's growing popularity made me all the more convinced that I had to find out why he was here.

Giving Charlie and Julie a brief nod, I grabbed my gear from the office and set up in the back of the studio where I could participate in the class without drawing attention to myself. The class began with a reading from a book of yoga meditations. Surprisingly, it was Charlie, not Julie, who read. His voice was low but clear, and he read as if he had an understanding of the author's message. After a standard warm-up session, we moved on to several of the traditional postures such as the Triangle, Warrior I and II, then the Pigeon. Once we were truly loosened up, to the point that my hip was starting to rebel after its afternoon spent in meditation, Julie led us into a series of variations of the Sun Salutation. We finished up on our backs doing some spinal twists. When Charlie dimmed the lights and we were covered with blankets for Savasana, I found my mind beginning to drift. Since I had expended so much effort earlier in the day in keeping my focus on the breath, I gave myself permission to let my mind wander.

I soon found it going back to one of its common themes: what life would have been like if the captain and I had been able to stay together. This had been a frequent fantasy of mine, and one that had gotten me through a number of difficult days in Iraq. There had been several variations: "The Captain and I" Versions 1.0, 1.1, and 1.2 had involved our becoming expatriates and travelling around Europe, spending the summers in England and the winters in Spain or the Cote d'Azur. "The Captain and I" Version 2.0 pictured us returning to the U.S. I had a number of versions here too, which ranged from the traditional house on a shady street with a white picket fence (not an image I was able to cling to for long, even in fantasy), to living in New York City, or alternatively, in a cottage along the rugged seacoast of northern Maine.

I was in touch with reality enough that every time I got a particular fantasy sharpened up to the point where I was about to propose it to the captain as a plan, some minor glitch, such as how we would earn a living, stopped me from suggesting it. I would then quickly embark on a new plan, which ended up being equally impractical.

Looking back now, I wondered what would have happened if I had worked up enough courage to actually make one of these proposals to the captain. I can picture him smiling and patting me on the head, as if I were a child who had said something amusing. I can also see him becoming even more agitated than he did when I broached the issue of what he would do after retirement.

I think what really worried him was that he had never formulated a plan for a future he saw rushing toward him, a future outside the military. Hell, he hadn't even divorced a wife whom he'd hardly seen during the previous ten years. The captain wasn't a planner. And the thought of having to take control of his own life filled him with fear. Why should that be surprising? Most men in the career military aren't in charge of their lives. That's one of the things that the military life provides for you: a structured life in which you are given a narrow range of options to choose from, and no matter which one you select, the fundamentals remain pretty much the same.

But what if I had taken the Army's place and planned out our future for him? Would the captain have then felt safe enough to begin on our life together? I had accused myself for a long time of having pushed him too far, to the point to which he got

us involved in that dangerous convoy to Baghdad. But maybe
the problem was that I hadn't pushed him enough. Could it be
he wanted someone who would tell him what to do just as the
Army had for twenty years, and if I had stepped into that role
more actively, we'd be together right now?

A sense of loss burned through me, still as strong as that day
on the road to Baghdad. I felt my fists clench at the thought of
what could never be. But then a small skeptical voice in the
back of my mind said, "Why didn't he tell you he was still married? Why did he lie to you?"

I'd mentioned this question to Izzy once.

"So why do you think he lied?" Izzy said.

"To get into my pants. He knew I wouldn't sleep with a married man."

"Is that the only reason?"

I'd shrugged. "Do you have a better one?"

"Maybe he loved you and knew he'd lose you if he told the
truth."

"Yeah," I'd responded with a snort.

But the more I thought about it, the more I'd decided it
really didn't matter. People lie as naturally as they breathe. They
lie as much to fool themselves as they do to fool others. I think
the captain wanted to hide from himself how much he still
wished he had a perfect marriage and family back in the States.
Even though his marriage was over, he refused to finally end it,
so he could sometimes imagine it was still there waiting for
him.

Not so different from Dr. Jim, who lied to himself about his
motives so he could continue believing he was a good person
who helped people rather than harmed them. Once the world
knew him as the killer of a small boy, he would have had to face
himself. Something he couldn't do.

Lying. We all do it. Like when I tell people I'm not in the

Army anymore because they'd virtually kicked me out because of my wounds. Not true. I had a choice. I could have stayed and finished out my time behind a desk. Maybe even reenlisted and continued my career in a less physical job. Possibly gone back to Iraq in some capacity or another. I had a choice, although I can barely admit it to myself. And I had chosen to leave because after the attack on that convoy, I just couldn't do it anymore.

A bell was struck three times, concluding deep relaxation. We slowly sat up and, after another reading by Charlie, we performed our Namastes. The lights were turned up again, and people began to leave, although a number remained to talk to Julie and Charlie. I waited until I saw him come out into the lobby.

"Charlie," I said, and waved him into my office.

He shuffled in with his head down as if he expected a beating.

"Good class," I said.

He nodded cautiously, waiting for the other shoe to drop. I felt guilty because I knew that was exactly what was going to happen.

"I'd like to keep you on here permanently. But I need to know some more about your past."

"Ananda says every day is a new beginning," he said tentatively.

"Right. But that doesn't mean we can completely ignore our yesterdays. Teaching yoga is a position of trust. I need to be certain I can trust you. Some of our students are rather impressionable."

"What do you want to know?"

"I want to know how you ended up at Ananda's center. I was there myself, you know, so I realize a pretty high percentage of the folks who wash up on that shore have a story to tell. I want to know yours."

"I killed my father."

I paused for a moment, wondering if this was the grim punch line to some joke, and I had missed the lead-in.

"I suppose that's hard for you to imagine," he went on.

Actually I had imagined it many times in vivid detail, but I wasn't about to share this bit of personal history with him.

"I can imagine a number of circumstances where a person might kill his father," I said carefully.

"He was a vicious man who used to beat me and my mom. So one day I killed him. I was sent to a juvenile detention center until I turned eighteen. I wandered around for a while after that until I ended up at Ananda's."

He stopped speaking and looked at me as if trying to read my reaction.

Julie appeared in the doorway. "Are you ready to go?" she asked Charlie. "I'm his ride for tonight, and I have to get home early," she explained.

"Okay, just give us a minute," I said to Julie. She glared at me as if I were abusing her cub. I glared back, and she drifted out of the doorway. I turned to Charlie. "Let's get together here tomorrow night at seven. I want to talk about this more after I've had the day to think about it."

Charlie nodded and shuffled off after Julie.

Twenty minutes later, after getting the records in order for who had paid, and locking what cash there was in the drawer, I headed back home. I pulled into the parking lot and walked up the outside stairs, still thinking about how I was going to handle the Charlie issue. I wasn't exactly the poster child for normality myself, but what if Charlie went off the rails and people got hurt?

"You knew he had killed his father, and you just let him teach?" I imagined Jack asking me in a tone of utter disbelief as we stood in my studio hip deep in bodies.

That didn't bear thinking about. No, I had to pursue the matter some more. How much more was the question. I was certain Ananda had sent Charlie to me because he thought I could help him. How he expected me to do that was the question.

I didn't stop thinking about Charlie until I looked down the second floor walkway that led to my condo. At one time this had been a motel, and it retained the same simple design, a first and second floor with open decks exposed to the parking lot below. I was at the end of the row in a small alcove that gave me a couple of side windows, a real benefit on a cloudy day. I noticed that the pool of light usually visible in the vicinity of my front door had been replaced by darkness. The management kept the lights burning all night for security, but that meant they often burned out, and unless a tenant complained, they were infrequently replaced. Since most tenants were short-term renters and couldn't be bothered, a substantial number of lights were out on any given night. Not usually mine, however, because I replaced the bulb as soon as it burned out.

I walked down the row toward my door, keeping my eyes open, ready to spot a figure lunging out of the darkness. I stepped into the alcove by my door, keeping my head turned in case someone came running up behind me. I stepped on something soft and stumbled forward, scratching my hand on the rough stucco wall I leaned on for support. Whatever I had stepped on groaned.

I leapt back and automatically went into a fighting stance.

"Who's there?" I asked.

"Is that you, Ali?"

"Who is it?"

"Me. Izzy." This time the response came from above the floor level, so I guessed he was getting to his feet.

"Izzy?" I said rushing forward. After a moment of fumbling, I managed to get my arm around him. With my free hand I worked the key into the lock. I flipped the ceiling light on, and helped him across the room, where he collapsed in one of the chairs in my small dining area.

A ribbon of blood flowed down Izzy's face from a cut in the left side of his scalp. His blue work shirt had dark stains from droplets of blood. He rubbed his right forearm and winced.

"What happened?" I called over my shoulder as I went into the bathroom for a wet cloth.

"I made the mistake of coming to visit you. I should have known that would get me into trouble."

"You were the one who wanted me to be more involved in life," I pointed out.

My comment silenced him for a moment. I came back with a damp cloth and began wiping away blood. He tried to take the cloth away from me and do the job himself, but I pointed out that this time I was the healer and he was the patient, Reiki Master or not. He relented. The gash on his head wasn't very deep, but, like most scalp wounds, it bled a lot. I asked him what was wrong with his arm, since he was rubbing it gingerly. He didn't answer me.

"I was trying to open the door to your apartment." He glanced up. "Do you know how hard it is to get a key in that lock when the light's out?"

I figured this for a rhetorical question.

"Well, it's damned hard. Anyway I was struggling with it when I heard this noise in the far corner by the side railing."

"The far corner?" That was on the opposite side from the stairs up to the third floor. It meant someone had to have been waiting there in the corner.

"Yeah. Then I heard feet running toward me, rubber soles slapping on the concrete. I turned. Couldn't really see anything, but something hit me on the head. I staggered backwards and automatically put my arm up. It's lucky I did because he took a second shot. Something hard glanced off my arm and hit me on the head again. I saw stars, but I managed to take a step forward and give whoever it was a pretty good shove backwards."

"Did your attacker say anything?"

"Nope."

"What happened after that?"

"I heard the bastard running away. I wanted to run after him, but suddenly I felt kind of woozy. That's all I remember until you started stepping on me."

I smiled. Being grumpy was a typical way men try to disguise a brush with danger. I'd done it myself.

"I knew I should never have encouraged you to give me a key to your place," Izzy said with a smile that told me he didn't mean it.

Two months ago Izzy had suggested I might give him a key. I'd been going through a rough patch, and I think he wanted to be able to get into my place without calling the police in case I dropped out of sight. Since I couldn't think of anyone else I'd rather have find my body, I had agreed.

"Why are you here?"

"You didn't answer your cell, so I figured that I'd come over here to check things out."

"I switched the phone off during class. Guess I forgot to turn it back on."

That brought a grunt in reply.

I rinsed out the cloth, put some ice in it, and gave it to Izzy to put on his head. He'd have a nice bump in the morning. I asked him if he wanted to go to the hospital to get some x-rays taken to check for a concussion. He gave me a look that suggested he definitely didn't. I asked about his arm and got the same response.

"So aside from checking to see if I was hanging from a light fixture, was there any other reason for this visit?"

"I got to thinking about this case you're investigating, and I wanted to find out how it was going."

"What you mean is, you read about Lauren's death in the paper and wanted to see how I was taking it."

He shrugged. "The people left behind often feel guilty when someone commits suicide, even if there was no way they could possibly have seen it coming."

"Yeah. Well, I've got a feeling Lauren's death might have been murder. I'm not sure how guilty I feel, but I am more determined than ever to get to the bottom of things."

"You think she was killed? By whom?"

I shrugged. "I'm not sure." I outlined for Izzy the sad story of Eddie Wolfe's death and the blackmail note.

"So what are you going to do next?"

"I'll see if I can find out what Lauren was up to for the past few days. If I can discover who she spoke to most recently, it may give me an idea about who killed her."

"Are you sure it was murder? It sounds to me like Lauren was pretty fragile. Maybe finding out about Dr. Jim pushed her over the edge. A big disappointment can do that."

I gave Izzy a look to let him know he wasn't exactly telling me anything I didn't already know about disappointment.

"I'll admit I don't have any proof. Jack hasn't gotten the lab work back on Lauren yet. But I think she was drugged before she was asphyxiated."

Izzy pushed himself out of the chair, leaning heavily on the table for support.

"I'm going to have the damned mother of all headaches," he said.

"Why don't I drive you to the hospital to get things checked out? You could have a concussion."

For the first time, I saw an expression of fear on Izzy's face.

"I don't like hospitals," he said quietly.

I nodded, knowing well enough not to press.

"Okay. If you have any problems in the night, give me a call."

"Yeah. But you know you're the one who should be careful. Whoever attacked me must have thought I was you. You figured that already, right?"

I nodded. "Whoever attacked you had loosened the bulb, so he could hide near the door. But that also meant he couldn't see who was putting the key in the lock and thought that I was coming home."

"Too bad I didn't get a better look at his face. This guy is probably Lauren's murderer, too."

"Probably."

"He was either figuring on scaring you off or hoping to put you permanently out of commission," Izzy said, giving me a long look to emphasize the importance of what he was saying.

"I'll be careful."

"Yeah," he grunted dubiously. "And you'd better let Jack know what happened in the morning."

"I could call him now. I'm sure he'd send a patrol car right over."

"Nah. I don't want to hang around answering a lot of questions. This isn't really about me anyway. It's about you and Lauren and Dr. Jim. But if Jack knows, maybe he can give you some backup."

We walked to the door and went out on the deck together. I reached over and turned the light bulb. The yellow light immediately came on.

"At least your killer is neat. He didn't smash the bulb and leave shards of glass all around," Izzy said.

"Neat and smart. Stepping on shattered glass might have been a giveaway."

Izzy turned to walk away. I resisted offering to escort him to his car.

"Call me if you need anything," I said. "And if you want to see me again in the next few days, it might be better if you gave me a call and we met at Larry's Lobster Shack."

Izzy smiled. "Yeah. Coming around here can be bad for a guy's health."

CHAPTER 19

The next morning was a preview of winter. The thermometer on my deck read just under forty, and a wicked wind blew across the tidal marsh. I had been looking forward to winter, which I'd pictured as a series of long walks on empty beaches with the frozen sand crystalline under my feet. If I was feeling well enough, I thought I might even get a dog to run with me for companionship. I could picture him darting into the waves, then looking back with a hurt expression as he realized how painfully cold the water could be.

But now, as I came inside from doing my Sun Salutations, bundled up in a heavy layer of sweats that smoothed out the angularity of my body, I felt differently. All I could picture was a long season spent scraping thick layers of ice off my car windshield and slipping and sliding my way across the parking lot to the studio. Our images of the future are usually rosier than the reality turns out to be.

After breakfast, I called the police station and discovered Jack was out but expected back by nine. I called Izzy just to be sure he hadn't suffered any ill effects from his attack. He had a headache and repeatedly warned me to be careful, but otherwise seemed none the worse for wear.

After spending a half-hour carefully cleaning the apartment in order to discipline my mind, I left for the police station. I walked in the front door, relieved to see a different sergeant was on duty today. Jack came down the hall with a mug in his hand and smiled.

"Want any coffee?" he asked waving me into his office. I declined and sat down, struggling to find a comfortable position in the molded plastic chair. By twisting so I was almost sitting sideways, I managed to find a spot where the pain was less noticeable.

"What did you find out at Carmody's Body Shop?" Jack asked, taking a sip of coffee.

My visit to Carmody's seemed so long ago, I'd almost forgotten about it. My face must have registered surprise because Jack asked, "That is what you came to talk about, isn't it?"

"It's not at the top of my list. Izzy, my Reiki Master, was attacked last night right outside my apartment."

Jack nodded. "Then he should come in and file a report."

"Yeah. Well, you see, the point is, I think the attacker thought Izzy was me. It was dark by the door, and Izzy was fumbling around with a key."

"He has a key to your apartment?" Jack asked, his jaw jutting out slightly.

"Somebody had to have a key in case I didn't answer the door."

Jack seemed about to ask a question, then a bleak expression came over his face and I figured he'd guessed the answer to his own question.

"Who would attack you?"

"Either Dr. Jim or his blackmailer." I went on to explain what I'd learned at Carmody's and my theory as to why Jim was being blackmailed.

When I was done, Jack said, "Let me get the Eddie Wolfe file to refresh my memory of the case."

I squirmed around on the hard chair and had just managed to find another barely tolerable position when Jack returned, glancing through an official-looking manila file.

"The newspaper account of the accident pretty much covered

everything we knew. The boy was riding his bicycle in the street after dark. His grandmother was in the front living room watching television. A car came along and hit the boy. The driver stopped suddenly. That much we could tell from the skid marks. The grandmother claimed he must have gotten out of the car because by the time she got to the door he was just getting back inside. Then he sped off. She said the car was a dark color, but that was all the information she could give us. We checked all the cars owned by folks in the neighborhood. None of them had damage that fit the accident."

"Why was Eddie living with his grandmother?"

"As far as we know from talking with the grandmother, his parents had split up. The grandmother, Mabel Wolfe, claimed the boy's mother had a drug problem and her son had divorced her because of the drugs."

"So why wasn't the boy with his father?"

"The grandmother wasn't very clear on that. I talked to her myself. She claimed her son was working all the time, so he couldn't be around the house enough to properly take care of his son."

"Sounds like a weak excuse."

Jack shrugged. "Hard to judge without more information. Maybe, now that he's single, the boy was in the way."

"Could we talk to the grandmother and see if she can tell us more about what happened?"

"Is she your most likely candidate for a blackmailer?"

"Granny could have seen more than she told you and decided to supplement her Social Security."

"Well, we can't talk to the grandmother. She died about two months ago. She fell down the cellar stairs."

I frowned.

"No reason to assume there must have been foul play," Jack said, reading my expression. "She was in her eighties and had a bad hip. It's an old house and the steps were a little tricky."

"So she couldn't have been the one putting the arm on the doc in September because she was dead in July. I hate when a good theory doesn't fit the facts."

Jack smiled. "Look, before we go out too far on a limb with this Eddie Wolfe thing, why don't we get a little more evidence that Dr. Jim is the guy who hit the kid."

"How are we going to do that?"

"Let's pay an official visit to Carmody's Body Shop. We sent out a bulletin to all body shops in the area right after the hit-and-run, telling them to be on the lookout for a car with damage to the front bumper and fender. Hitting a kid would leave a pretty big dent. If Carmody failed to report something, we might be able to get some more information out of him."

"Sounds like a good plan to me."

This time I breezed right past Dave, who stood at the counter gaping at us. Jack simply waved his badge at him and said we'd find our own way to Mr. Carmody's office. The secretary whom I had pegged as being Mrs. Carmody went from polite to angry to scared in a matter of a few seconds as we said who we were and then marched past her and down the hall to her husband's office. When we entered the office, I thought Carmody's already wrinkled face instantly added a few more lines. Gamely he got to his feet and shook hands with both of us.

"I just wanted to follow up on a couple of things you told Ms. Randall."

Carmody nodded. His heavy chin seemed to recede even further into his barrel chest, like a turtle that dearly wanted to slide back inside its shell.

"You said Dr. Schianno came to you because he could get a lower rate here than he could elsewhere. This was based on the fact that he had diagnosed your heart problems when another doctor hadn't."

"That's right."

"So the bill the doctor paid for two hundred dollars was substantially less than the work was worth."

"Very substantially."

"What did he have done?"

"I'll have to check my records again."

"Why don't you do that," Jack suggested.

Carmody got to his feet and slowly maneuvered down the hall as if he were walking through deep water. Jack glanced at me and winked. I could hear urgent whispering down the hall between Carmody and his wife/secretary. Her higher pitched whispers sounded angry. When Carmody returned, he dropped the file on the desk and didn't even bother to open it.

"I pretty much know what's in there. Why don't you ask your questions and I'll answer all of them I can."

Jack nodded. "What was the damage to the doctor's car?"

"The right front bumper and fender were dented."

"How serious was the damage?"

"Pretty bad."

"Was there any sign of blood or hair in the area of damage?"

Carmody nodded. "Dr. Jim said he'd hit a large dog."

"And you believed him?" Jack asked, allowing sarcasm to seep into his voice.

"I had no reason to disbelieve him. How was I supposed to know otherwise?"

"Maybe by checking the police notice we had sent out about a hit-and-run in Cornwall the night before. Or don't you bother to read those?"

"I saw it. That's why I asked the doctor if he was sure it was a dog he hit."

"And what did he say?" I asked.

"He told me the animal ran off, but he was sure it was a dog."

"And you believed him?" Jack asked again. "Didn't you think the damage was suspicious enough that you should have reported it to us and let the police determine if he was telling the truth?"

Carmody sighed. "Look, the doc had saved my life. I thought he was an honest guy. I didn't want to offend him by asking a lot of questions and implying he was a liar. Sure I had a few doubts when he said he'd hit a dog, but how was I to know he was lying? And I wasn't about to put the police onto him after all he'd done for me."

Jack got to his feet. "Ms. Randall tells me you just got back from a vacation."

"Yeah."

"Don't take any long trips for a while without notifying me. You're now a witness in an ongoing homicide investigation."

As we went out the door, I saw the secretary standing at the end of the hall where she could probably have picked up everything we'd been saying.

"Do you have anything to add?" Jack asked as we walked past her.

"We'll stay right here in town as long as you need us," she promised.

He grunted and kept walking.

Jack was silent for the first part of the ride back to town. Finally he turned to me and said, "I have less use for people like that than I do for a crook."

"People like what?" I asked.

"Your good average citizen who can't be bothered to help the police."

"I can understand why he didn't blow the whistle on the doc."

"Yeah. You do me a favor, I do one for you. And the hell with what happens to society."

I knew I should keep quiet, but the subject was a hobbyhorse of mine.

"Society is an abstraction. Loyalty is something you owe to people. Carmody felt he owed Dr. Jim. I can respect his believing that he had to pay him back."

Jack turned to me. "So you're saying he was right not to let us know about the doc's damaged car?"

I shook my head. "I'm just saying I can understand it."

"Would you have done the same thing?"

"I don't know. There are limits to loyalty."

We didn't talk again after that until we got back to the parking lot at the police station. Jack didn't open the door right away, so I stayed seated, staring straight ahead.

"Dr. Jim's disappearance is now part of a hit-and-run investigation. So you'd better back off now, Alison."

I knew this was more than a request.

"You wouldn't even know Dr. Jim was involved in Eddie Wolfe's death if it wasn't for me. Don't you think that you owe me a little slack?"

"This isn't a question of personal feelings. It was pretty informal up to now, because we didn't know if Dr. Jim's disappearance was part of anything criminal. We have reason to think so now, and I'm asking you to back off."

"I understand what you're asking."

"Are you going to do it?"

"I can't."

"Why not?"

"For one reason, someone out there is trying to kill me because of what I've already uncovered. I'm not going to sit back and hope the Cornwall Police Department kicks into gear fast enough to prevent another attempt on my life."

"Is that the only reason?"

I paused for a moment, wondering how much truth I owed Jack.

"No," I finally admitted. "I also owe it to Lauren. She came to me for help, and even though I didn't want to give it, I finally agreed. And so her death is partly my fault."

"It could have been suicide."

"I'll believe that when I hear the medical examiner's report."

"Another two days," Jack said.

"Until then, I act as if it's murder."

"And you keep on investigating?"

I nodded.

"Another one of these issues of personal loyalty?"

"In a way."

Jack shook his head and got out of the car.

"Try to stay out of trouble, Alison," he called across the hood as I turned away.

I answered with a wave.

CHAPTER 20

Leaving the police station parking lot, I decided I had once again allowed speculation to race ahead of fact. I had leapt to the conclusion that Dr. Jim must have been the driver of the car that hit Eddie Wolfe, without carefully checking out the scene of the crime. No doubt Jim's story about hitting a large dog appeared weak, but dogs did sometimes wander into the road. A drive up and down Lauren's street would help me to determine whether Jim would normally have driven the route past the Wolfe house.

Once out of the parking lot I went down to Route 1 and headed north. Half a mile later I turned right on Ocean Street. Aptly named, the street is the fastest way to the beach because it goes directly across Cornwall and dead-ends at the beach. In the other direction it goes out toward the medical clinic where Jim had worked. Traveling even farther out you would eventually arrive at the neighborhood where he lived with his wife and family. If you drove toward the ocean, you soon went past the street leading to the condo development where Jim had lived after his separation. A mile later, Lauren's street, Hazlett Terrace, was a left turn off Ocean about a block before reaching the sand. So this would most likely have been the route Dr. Jim would have traveled from Lauren's place to wherever else he might have gone.

Ocean is also the main street of Cornwall. Right where it bisects Route 1 there are a couple of blocks of shops, pizzerias, gas stations, and liquor stores. As you keep going toward the beach, the stores fade away into residences and a sprinkling of bed and breakfast places. By the time I turned onto Hazlett, the homes had become older and more faded. Someday in the not too distant future, this part of town would be redeveloped to appeal to the tourist trade, as was happening up and down the East Coast whenever you are within hearing distance of the surf. So far, however, Cornwall had remained just outside the scope of change. A few condos had sprung up during the boom time of the nineties, but it would take another period of economic growth before Cornwall would be drastically changed. Then I'd probably have to move on again.

I made a left onto Lauren's street. Going slowly so that I could read the numbers, I found the Wolfe house. It was the third house on my left, a tired two story with a small glassed-in front porch. There was no house directly across the street, and the neighbors on either side were set back from the road. It would have taken a very alert neighbor with good vision to spot very much on the night of Eddie's death. If the grandmother had made it out onto the porch in time, however, she might have seen something.

I traveled up the street. I hadn't been counting on the night of Lauren's death, but her house was the sixth and last but one on the odd-numbered side of the street. The street ended in a stand of stunted pines and then tidal marsh. One side street came into Lauren's street on the left. I went back and followed it out. Three more streets formed a little neighborhood that looked to be a decade newer than the houses on Hazlett. But to reach Ocean Street and go anywhere, you would have to drive down to Hazlett, then out past Eddie Wolfe's house. Since Jack told me the police had checked every car in the neighborhood, the driver must have been a visitor at someone's home or a driver who happened to be cruising the neighborhood.

I made a circle and returned to drive back down Hazlett, once more taking a look at the Wolfe house. The street lights were far apart, the nearest one a good two hundred feet from where Eddie had been riding his bike. I imagined he would have been very hard to see if someone was driving the least bit too fast or was slightly preoccupied. I could visualize Dr. Jim stopping the car, quickly ascertaining the boy was seriously injured, then seeing the light come on in the glassed-in porch. In that instant he made the fateful decision to drive away rather than wait for the police.

I turned around and went up the street, planning to take one more look at Lauren's house. I wasn't sure what I expected to find. Before I got there, however, I saw a woman I knew raking leaves in the side yard of the house on the left. It was Sarah Contell, my yoga student. Normally I would have driven past, feeling lucky she hadn't spotted me. A friendly wave wouldn't have been enough if she did see me. I'd have to stop and talk with her or probably lose a customer. But this time I willingly pulled up at the curb and got out of the car. She glanced over at me, hearing the door slam. At first Sarah's expression was one of puzzlement. She probably didn't recognize me outside of the yoga context. Then the penny dropped and she smiled.

"Ali, how good to see you," she called over the hedge separating her property from the road.

I tried to return the greeting with similar enthusiasm. She came over to the sidewalk that led up to her house and waved me toward her.

Before I could frame a question, she said, "I've just about had it with raking these leaves for the day. Why don't you come inside and I'll make us a cup of tea? I'm sure a person who practices yoga as seriously as you would prefer green tea. But I'm afraid that all I've got is black or chamomile."

I followed her around the house and to the side door, which led into the kitchen. Since Sarah had to be pushing eighty, I expected to see a kitchen from my childhood, with yellow appliances, metal counter tops, and a simple wooden table. Instead it was a dazzling contemporary kitchen. Dark green granite made up every counter surface, and stainless steel appliances dominated the back wall. A large island stood in the center with chairs lined up along the gleaming countertop. I could see a table in the dining room made of smoked glass, which featured an abstract metal sculpture in the center.

Sarah looked at my face, enjoying my expression of surprise. "It has that effect on everyone. I guess folks expect that, since I'm getting older, I wouldn't see any point in buying anything new because I won't have much chance to use it, but I come from long-lived stock, and I figure I have at least a good ten years left, so why not enjoy things if I can afford them."

I nodded.

"That's why I started yoga. After all, just because my body has a few miles on it doesn't mean I shouldn't take care of it."

She waved me to a chair along the counter and put on the water kettle. I got a clear impression that if I wanted her full attention, it would be best to wait until she had arranged everything the way she wanted it and sat down. Sarah began rummaging around in a pantry closet and soon returned with a box of store-bought cookies.

"In spite of having this fancy kitchen, I'm not much of a cook. Never was. And living alone as I do since Mr. Contell passed, I don't spend much time around the house. I'd rather be out and around people."

She arranged the cookies on a plate just as the water began to whistle.

"Black or chamomile?" she asked.

"Black."

She nodded agreement. "Right. No sense getting too relaxed this early in the day."

She got out two mugs and one tea bag.

"Do you mind sharing a tea bag?" she asked. "I don't like my tea very strong."

"Fine."

"Milk or lemon?" she asked when both cups were filled with a rather weak brew.

"No."

"Good."

Finally she settled down across from me, took a sip of tea, and smiled.

"Well, I assume you didn't come out here just to have a cup of tea with me. What brings you to the neighborhood?"

Startled by her directness, it took me a second to open my mouth to answer, but she raised a hand to silence me.

"That was silly of me. I already know the answer: Lauren."

"How did you know?"

I could have sworn she gave a slightly guilty blush.

"Actually, the night Lauren died I heard all the commotion with the ambulance and police cars. Being a curious kind of person, I couldn't help but go up and take a look at what was going on. I saw you there leaning against the police car. I kind of got into a conversation with one of the officers there, a very nice young man, and he told me what had happened."

"And you figured that because I found her I'd be back in the neighborhood?" I asked, puzzled.

She shook her head, then hesitated a moment as if unsure whether to say anything more.

"No. I figured you'd be back here because you were helping Lauren find out what happened to her fiancé."

"How did you know that?"

"Lauren came to see me in the early afternoon of the day she died. She told me you had been helping her."

I took another sip of tea and studied Sarah for a moment. I could see now that I'd badly misjudged her. I'd written her off as a foolish old lady who had time and money enough to dabble in yoga and probably a host of other hobbies. But, although she might be a dabbler, she was no fool.

"Were you and Lauren friends?"

"Not really. I'd seen her around the yoga studio from time to time over the last few months. We'd say hello and talk about the weather. Before I started taking yoga, the only time I saw her was when she would walk past the house. She was a great one for talking walks on the beach, and she had to go up the street to get to the beach access. And she stopped by one time to ask me if I was interested in selling my house because she had a client who was looking for a place in the neighborhood. I told her I wouldn't know where else to go if I moved. She said she would help me with that if I ever changed my mind."

"Why did Lauren come to see you on the day she died?"

"She wanted to find out what I knew about Eddie Wolfe's death."

"Did she say why she wanted to know?"

"No. And I didn't ask her. She seemed upset, and I didn't think it was any of my business why she wanted to know."

"Were you home when the boy got hit?"

"Yes. I didn't know anything had happened until I heard the sirens when the police showed up. I walked down the street to see what was going on."

I figured she must have been the witness Jack had mentioned.

"Did you talk to anyone?" I asked.

Sarah nodded. "Mabel Wolfe. Mabel was trying to tell the police what had happened, but she was crying so much, she hardly made any sense. One of the officers asked me to see if I could calm her down enough to get a coherent description of what had taken place."

"Were you able to?"

Sarah nodded. "She stopped crying eventually. Personally, I think a lot of her bawling was just for show."

"Why do you say that?" I asked, surprised.

"She reeked of alcohol. Of course, that didn't surprise me much. Everyone in the neighborhood knew she drank. We were all a little surprised her son would have sent Eddie to stay with her."

"He lives somewhere up north?"

Sarah nodded. "Somewhere in northern Vermont. Her son broke up with his wife, and for some reason Mabel ended up taking care of the boy."

"Did Mabel actually see anything at the time of the accident?"

"At first I thought she had. She said something to me about a dark-colored car pulling away right after she went out on the porch. I got the impression Mabel was about to tell me something more about it when she stopped and got this sort of cagey look in her eye." Sarah paused. "There was always a shifty side to Mabel. She lived on the street for thirty years, and kind of kept to herself even when her husband was alive. I guess a lot of heavy drinkers isolate themselves. But over the years I've talked to her quite a few times, and I have to say I never cared for her much. There was something sneaky about her."

From the way she said the word "sneaky" I could tell sneakiness was a major fault according to Sarah.

"You have no idea what she was about to tell you?"

"Nope. I just figured it was something about the car because that was what we had just been talking about. Then this expression came over her face like she'd suddenly come up with a brilliant idea."

An idea for blackmail, I thought to myself.

"Did you tell Lauren all of this?"

"I did. She wanted to know if I had any idea where she could get more information about the accident. I told her I didn't. With Mabel dead and the police not knowing any more than she told them, I figured there wasn't much more to find out. She wanted to know if any of the other neighbors might have seen something, and I told her I was the only neighbor who showed up that night. I think the people across the street were out, and the folks on either side of Mabel use their houses seasonally. There are only ten houses on this street, and I think just four are lived in year round."

I sipped my tea and tried a cookie. It was stale. I wondered whether Lauren had figured, as I did, that Mabel Wolfe had planned to blackmail Dr. Jim. But Jack was right about the timing being off. Dr. Jim had received his blackmail note in September, and Mabel had died before then.

"Do you remember exactly when Mabel died?"

Sarah nodded. "Right after the Fourth of July. It was during the same week." A smile flitted across the woman's face. "I remember having the unkind thought that perhaps she'd been celebrating the country's independence a little too much, and that's why she fell."

"Do you know who found her body?"

"That was an odd thing. The people next door were renters, and the man came over to ask her if she knew where they had to go to get beach permits. Mabel's back door was open, and he saw that there was food on the table, as if somebody was eating a meal. He went inside the kitchen and the door to the cellar was open. He looked down the stairs and saw her body. He was a young guy from Boston, so I guess he didn't mind barging into someone's house. Of course, it was a good thing he did, or else she could have lain there undiscovered for weeks."

"Had she been dead long?"

"The police officer I talked to said they thought her fall happened the day before."

I smiled to myself at Sarah's skill in getting information out of the police. I guess they figured there was no harm in telling things to their grandmother. Jack probably wouldn't be happy to hear about it, but I didn't intend to tell him.

"Did Lauren ask you anything else?"

Sarah paused. "Yes. She asked me if I knew whether Mabel had owned her house. I told her she did. Then Lauren asked if I knew what was going to happen to it now that Mabel was dead. I told her I figured that it would be sold once her estate was settled. As far as I knew she only had one child, Edward, so he'd probably end up selling it. She asked me if I had his address or phone number, and I told her I didn't."

"Have you ever met Edward?"

"I knew him when he was a boy. But I've only seen him once since he went away to college over fifteen years ago, and that was at Eddie's funeral. But I don't think he stayed around long. I guess he came back again for his mother's funeral, but I didn't go. I thought about it, because she was a neighbor and all, but finally I decided I wasn't going to try to say nice things about someone I really didn't like. Plus it conflicted with my Pilates class."

I drained the last of my tea, trying to think of anything else to ask.

"Did you and Lauren talk about anything else?"

"Nothing important. As she was leaving, we sort of commented on the fact that we'd never have gotten to know each other if we hadn't received those flyers in our mailboxes about your yoga studio."

Those damned flyers again.

"How many people got them?" I asked.

"I don't know," Sarah replied, as if that was something I should know. "But I think everyone on this street did. One of my neighbors mentioned it. It was a great promotion. You should do it again some time."

I nodded, figuring I would if I could remember having done it the first time. We walked out the door together and down to the street.

I paused by my car. "Did Lauren say anything about what she was going to do next?"

"No. But she seemed to have something on her mind."

Sarah paused and looked across the street, where you could see the ocean peeking over a berm of sand. "You know, I never cared much for Lauren. She was always a bit high strung for my taste and a bit too aggressive with her real estate talk. But if I'd ever thought she was upset enough to take her own life, I would have let somebody know."

I reached out, stopping just short of touching Sarah's arm.

"I would have, too," I said.

CHAPTER 21

From Sarah's place I went back home and had a late lunch: a piece of toast and a cup of tea. My stomach didn't seem up to much more than that. When I looked outside, the day had once again gone downhill. The sky was gunmetal gray and the air chilly and blustery. But I put on a fleece workout jacket and went out, determined to get in my walk on the beach, regardless of conditions. I figured I'd better toughen myself up now, because the weather was going to be a lot worse in winter.

I drove down to the beach parking lot. There were only a couple of cars, unlike the summer when it would be full by early afternoon. I looked up and down the beach. There were two people up the beach on my left about a half-mile away heading in the opposite direction, and three on the right heading toward me. I decided to go out in the direction of the people who were moving away, not feeling in the mood to muster even a polite nod of the head in passing.

I began walking at a fast clip, spending the first five minutes focusing on my body. One of the things I had learned from Ananda is to do a daily full-body scan, which is nothing more than doing some simple exercise with full awareness of how each part of your body feels. Sounds simple, like how can we not be conscious of how our body feels? But as Ananda would frequently point out, we tend to suppress unpleasant sensations as we go through the day. Wanting to get things done, we ignore the tensions and pains in various parts of our body. Only when something reaches the level of acute pain do we grant it recognition, and by then it's likely some permanent damage has been done.

As I walked along, I realized my bad hip felt surprisingly good. It had been a bit achy since my altercation in the lumberyard, which had probably stressed it too much. But today it seemed to be better than normal. There was a little stiffness in the right side of my neck, which could be the result of sleeping with my head twisted, a problem I frequently had. I also had some tension around the eyes I attributed to my morning spent investigating. I've concluded that when I'm talking to witnesses, I must stare at them with unusual intensity, because I come away with the same kind of eyestrain I get after a couple of hours spent battling with my computer. I gently twisted my neck to relieve the pressure and consciously tried to relax my face and eyes, focusing on a distant point up the beach. After five minutes, I was ready to think about the case again.

I was still working on the assumption that Lauren had been murdered and was not a suicide. If that was the case, then something she found out must have made her killer believe she was too dangerous to leave alive. What had she found out from Sarah Contell? Nothing that made Dr. Jim look any guiltier of the hit-and-run. She already knew when he had left her house and when Eddie had been killed, so once I told her about the blackmail note, she must have concluded Jim had lied to her about hitting the boy, assuming she had ever asked him. Aside from the grandmother, who apparently wasn't willing to tell everything she knew, there were no eyewitnesses. As far as I could see, Lauren didn't know about Jim's trip to Carmody's Body Shop, although in retrospect she may have viewed his sudden decision to sell his BMW as a sign of guilt.

Could she have been a threat to Dr. Jim in some way? I didn't see her going to the police and attempting to get them to open an investigation into Jim's involvement in the accident. Although no doubt disappointed in the good doctor, I figured she still loved him and would want to discuss the matter with him before going to the cops. This conclusion led to another question: could she have contacted him in some way? If she had been part of his scheme to disappear, she would know how to reach him. I had already rejected that idea because if she were part of Dr. Jim's plot, she wouldn't have involved me.

Was there any reason Dr. Jim would have suddenly decided to get in touch with her? I could imagine him calling from out of the blue and coming up with a plausible story about why he had to disappear. With a little more of a stretch, I could even picture him convincing her that she was imagining his involvement in the hit-and-run. She might even have invited him to her house to talk, giving him the perfect opportunity to kill her. But I didn't see how Dr. Jim, wherever he was hiding, could know she was digging into the death of Eddie Wolfe. And if he did know, he'd have to kill me, too. I stood still for a moment, having surprised myself. Someone had tried to kill me just last night, one night after Lauren's death. Could Dr. Jim have found out that Lauren and I were getting close to discovering his vehicular homicide?

But how would Jim have found out? His wife could have told him I was asking questions at Lauren's behest, I thought. Maybe he called her instead of Lauren and fed her a convincing story that got her to forgive and forget, which easily led to aid and abet. She could have been his information conduit. Maybe he was planning to start over somewhere new with his wife and family once his criminal act was in no danger of coming out.

"You're forgetting something important," a voice in my head said in a mocking tone. "You're forgetting the blackmailer. The blackmailer would still know what he had done and could call the authorities if he ran away."

I turned around and began walking back the way I had come. The wind was in my face now, causing my cheeks to burn and my eyes to water. My little voice was right. I had forgotten about the blackmailer. How would it help Dr. Jim to eliminate Lauren and me if the blackmailer was still out there with incriminating information? A letter to the authorities from an anonymous source would probably be enough to get the police looking into things, and Jim had to know they would pretty quickly find their way to Carmody's Body Shop. And I figured a scorned blackmailer would be as angry as a scorned girlfriend or wife, and probably a whole lot harder for Dr. Jim to sweet talk.

I was pretty much back to where I had started, both physically and mentally, so I walked across the sand and back to my car. I always leave my cell phone in the car when I walk on the beach. No one has to reach me urgently, or at least no one should if they're leading the proper yogic lifestyle and letting the universe provide. As soon as I slid in behind the wheel, it began to ring as if to reprimand me for leaving it alone in the cold car while I was enjoying a romp on the beach.

"This is Jack. Glad I finally got you, I've been calling for the last twenty minutes."

"I was taking a walk on the beach."

"You're lucky you can get time off during the day."

"It's a lifestyle choice."

"Well, I've got some news for you. I think we've found Dr. Jim."

"Where was he hiding?"

"Well, he wasn't exactly hiding. Some fishermen hauled him on board in their nets off the coast of Cape Cod. A real stroke of luck for us, although not for them, I imagine. A one in a million shot, maybe more. I'm in the car right now heading down to Boston with his dental records to see if we can get a positive ID."

"You're going yourself? Couldn't you just fax them?"

"I figure being on the scene will cut through a couple of days of paperwork."

"After all that time in the water, is there any reason to think that it's him?" I'd never actually seen a floater, but I'd heard enough stories about how you wouldn't recognize your own mother under those circumstances, not that I would recognize mine anyway.

Jack was silent for a moment. "He had an unusual tattoo on his right shoulder. Apparently much of it was still recognizable."

"You didn't mention a tattoo to me," I said, trying not to sound too reproachful. After all, I wasn't officially part of the investigation.

"We have to hold stuff like that back from the public."

So I'd gone from being virtually part of the team to being John Q. Citizen. Actually, I realized with a bitter taste in my mouth, I'd probably never been much more than that, except for when I had been useful to Jack.

"What was the nature of this 'unusual' tattoo?"

"A caduceus."

"Really? I guess he took this medical stuff pretty seriously."

"A lot of cops have tattoos of handcuffs," Jack offered.

Where's yours, I wanted to ask, but decided I really didn't want to be so personal.

"How did he die?"

"We'll have to wait on the medical examiner for a determination on cause of death. We can't even be sure how long he's been dead, although the guy from the Coast Guard I talked to on the phone said it would have taken a while for him to get so far out to sea. In fact, he wouldn't have gotten that far out if he'd just walked into the ocean."

"What does that mean?"

"According to my Coast Guard friend, he must have been at

least a quarter of a mile out when he went in the water."

Neither one of us said anything for a few seconds.

"Are you thinking what I'm thinking?" Jack finally asked.

"I am if it has anything to do with a woman in a wetsuit with a surfboard."

"Yeah, just what I was thinking. She kills the doc then puts his body on the surfboard and heads out to sea. She dumps him beyond the tide line and comes back, pretty confident the body will never be found."

"So the person who wrote the letter wasn't really a black-mailer; she was just setting him up for murder," I said.

"Or else Dr. Jim was reluctant to pay, tried to do away with her, and lost."

"And she just happened to have her surfboard handy to take his body out to sea. No, this sounds like it was planned. She went there intending to kill him. She lured him there with the blackmail note, but money wasn't what she was interested in getting."

"What was it that she wanted?"

"Revenge." I wasn't quite sure where that came from, but it suddenly sounded right to me.

"Finally one of his girlfriends didn't buy into his 'you'll be better off without me speech'?"

"Maybe. I'm not sure. I was halfway certain Dr. Jim was the one who had killed Lauren and clobbered Izzy last night, so I have more thinking to do."

I heard Jack clear his throat as if he were arriving at a deci-sion to be unprofessional.

"Well, I guess you deserve to know. You were right about Lauren. I've got the tox screen on her, and she was full of barbiturates and alcohol."

"Could she have taken them herself?"

"Not unless she disposed of the drug bottles. No prescription bottles matching the drugs in her system were found at the scene."

"And it couldn't have been Dr. Jim who gave them to her," I said.

"Long dead by then."

"Thanks for telling me about Lauren."

"You deserved to know. And I'm sorry I got kind of stiff when we were driving back from Caromody's. I get a little nervous when people start talking about deciding what laws to uphold and which ones to break."

"Yeah. I can understand that. But you should know I have a rogue side to me."

Jack laughed. "Only one."

I caught myself smiling out the car window. A woman walking past with her boyfriend looked in at me and began pulling on his arm as if she couldn't get away fast enough.

"Fair enough," I said. "I'll give you a call if I come up with any bright ideas about our mystery woman."

"I'll let you know if I find out anything more."

We broke the connection and I drove back to my place. I was sad to hear Dr. Jim was gone. He'd had a good touch with the scalpel, and he had treated me better than most in his profession. I was angrier than ever about Lauren, now that I knew that she had definitely been murdered. But I also felt surprisingly happy that Jack and I seemed to be back on friendly terms. I knew Izzy would be pleased about it, too. He's always telling me that I have to "pierce my shell of self-imposed isolation," which sounds to me like a chicken being hatched. When I respond it's the shell that keeps me safe, he shakes his head vigorously and says that rather than protecting me, it's slowly suffocating me. Just proves one man's suffocation is another woman's safety.

As if on cue my phone rang again, and it was Izzy. Debunkers of parapsychology say the idea is nonsense that our thinking about someone stimulates them into getting in touch with us. It's bound to happen occasionally based on sheer probability, and we simply forget all the times we think about someone and never hear from them. So we turn the exception into some kind of rule. Fair enough, but it's still pretty eerie when it happens.

"Hey," Izzy bellowed in my ear, which told me he was in his car, an old Pontiac rattletrap that forced him to shout to be heard. "I'm on my way to see a client, so I can't talk long. But I remembered something about last night."

"The name of your assailant?"

"Funny, Randall. If I didn't know better, I'd say you were in a good mood. What I wanted to tell you is, I think the person who attacked me was shorter than I am."

"Why do you think that?"

"Well, I remembered the guy who hit me raised whatever it was up over his head, and when he brought it down, he hit me on the forehead just below the hairline. I'm five-ten, so that means whoever hit me was probably way shorter than that or he'd have hit me higher up, toward the top of my head."

"Sounds logical. Anything else?"

Izzy laughed. "What? You want me to solve the case for you? Where's the challenge in that?"

"Thanks for the information."

"Are you making any progress?"

I told him about the police being certain Lauren was murdered and about the discovery of Dr. Jim's body. A loud whistle came down the line in response.

"So you figure the same person killed them both?"

"Yeah. And I'm guessing it was the woman that was at the beach that night. The one Harry Link saw."

"Any idea who she is?"

"None at all."

"So what are you going to do next?"

"Go home and think."

"About what?"

"About what Lauren did between her visit with Sarah Contell in the afternoon and her death later on the same day."

"You think she found out something that got her killed?"

"More than that. She either directly contacted her killer or got in touch with someone who clued the killer in to the fact that Lauren was onto her."

"If you figure out what Lauren did, then what are you going to do?"

"I plan to do the same thing myself."

"So you can end up just like Lauren?" Izzy said.

"No. There's a difference. Lauren didn't know what she was bringing down on herself. I'll be aware of what I'm doing."

I got a skeptical silence from the other end of the line.

"Do you feel like doing a little more dancing tonight?"

"Is your head up to it?" I asked.

"I don't dance on my head like those hip-hop guys. So I'll be fine."

"Okay. A little break from the case might be a good idea. But I'm meeting Charlie tonight around seven at the studio to talk about things, and I've got a little paperwork to do."

"Why don't I meet you at the studio at seven-thirty? We can leave one car in the lot in front of your place. The band starts up at eight, and it gets kind of crowded in the bar parking lot on dance night."

"Sounds like a plan."

By the time Izzy and I rang off, I was pulling in the parking lot of my condo. Walking in the wind, or maybe it was all that thinking, had given me an appetite, and I was looking forward to throwing together some dinner.

CHAPTER 22

Throwing together dinner turned out to be an accurate description. Some leftover tuna fish and a few remaining chickpeas got tossed on top of some lettuce leaves I sprinkled with extra virgin olive oil. I added a few stale crackers I found in the back of the cabinet to provide some crunch. I try to eat one good meal a day. I wake up every morning telling myself I'm going to do that. Unfortunately life always seems to get in the way. And to be honest, I'm just not much of a cook. Not having a resident mother meant I never learned cooking at the time in life when at least some girls do.

My father always seemed to hire cooks who preferred to work their magic alone, away from the prying eyes of children. In the Army, the mess hall usually provided all I needed. Unlike many, I never had a problem with Army food; it tasted pretty good and was filling. Now I find myself lacking the motivation to learn cooking skills just for myself, and the chances of my ever having to cook for two are about as likely as my opening a four-star restaurant.

As soon as I began to eat, my mind drifted back to the case. Fifteen minutes later I looked down to see that my plate was empty, and I couldn't recall having eaten. These lapses in attention are one of the more disturbing remnants of my adventure in Iraq. Some doctors saw it as the lingering result of a concussion; a scarier view was that for some reason I was having mini-strokes and blacking out in the middle of normal activities. But there was no physical proof for either of these theories, although to be fair, I'd checked myself out of the hospital and the Army before the planned battery of tests could be run. The Army shrink who spoke with me for a fifty-minute hour claimed I was suffering from post-traumatic stress that caused images from the past to block out the present, but these images were so disturbing, I was later unable to recall them. Hence my Swiss cheese—like memory. The shrink's notion sounded a little too complicated for me, as though he were trying to fit me to some pet theory.

Izzy's simple explanation was that I had developed a blink-ered approach to life. I focused my attention like a laser on whatever interested me, while everything else receded into the shadows. I liked his view better because at least it implied I was capable of clear, although narrow, thought.

So what had my mind been focused on while I was appar-ently putting down chickpeas and tuna? Well, I was trying to figure out what Lauren had done after she had visited Sarah Contell. Her last questions to Sarah about Mabel had concerned the house and who had inherited it. A sensible query from a realtor, but how would she have followed up on it? She knew Dr. Jim had been unusually worried during the week before he disappeared, and she might have suspected the possibility of blackmail. She would also have known Mabel Wolfe was the most likely person to have seen Dr. Jim leave the scene of the accident, but she also knew Mabel died in July.

I figured Lauren's next question, as mine was right now, concerned the person with whom Mabel might have shared her secret. Sarah had said that as a reclusive alcoholic, Mabel had no real friends, and if she did have friends, she'd be unlikely to tell them about information she'd withheld from the police for the purpose of blackmail. Would she have told her son? Maybe she did, and he took up the role of blackmailer after his mother's accident on the cellar stairs. Or possibly he wanted vengeance more than money and decided to use the information he had to get Dr. Jim to meet him in a secluded spot where he could murder him. This idea sounded pretty good to me except for the fact that Edward Wolfe had been happy to board his son with his grandmother and had shown little apparent interest in the boy. He had made a perfunctory trip down to Cornwall when his son died, but hadn't stayed around to urge the police on to greater efforts. This didn't sound like the stuff from which revenge is made.

Who did that leave? I asked myself, as I finished chewing the last mouthful of my forgotten lunch. Now I sat at the table staring at my plate and trying to convince myself I should feel full, whereas all I felt was woefully lacking in information. I was so surprised by the answer that came to me, I sat there with my mouth hanging open.

"You talk all the time about your father and your stepbrothers," Izzy had once said to me. "But you never mention your mother."

"There's not much to say."

"Why not?"

"I hardly remember her."

"Why is that?"

"She went away," I had answered, pressing my lips together firmly so no other words would slip out.

"Went away where?"

I shrugged. "California. That's what my father told us anyway."

"Did you try to get in touch with her?"

"I was only a year old when she left."

"I mean later on."

"She wouldn't have wanted to hear from me."

"How do you know that?"

"She never tried to get in touch with me. Even when I was a kid, she never called or sent a card on my birthday. I figured she didn't want anything to do with me."

"Did she get in touch with your brothers?"

I shook my head. "My brothers blamed me because she left shortly after I was born. They said if I'd never been born, our mother wouldn't have left."

Izzy had taken another bite of his taco and looked out over the tidal marsh. After a long moment he spoke. "Maybe she didn't get in touch with you because she felt guilty about leaving you. Maybe she was afraid to get in touch with you because she thought you didn't love her anymore."

"She'd have been right," I replied.

But just because my mom had forgotten about me didn't mean the same was true of Eddie Wolfe's mom. I'd assumed, because she had broken up with her husband and Eddie had ended up with his paternal grandmother, his mother had permanently left the scene and lost any further interest in what happened to her son. But such wasn't necessarily the case. When she heard about her son's death, she might have wanted to find out what had happened to him. And where would she have gone for that information? Right to Mabel Wolfe, the woman responsible for her son's welfare and the one who was on the scene when he had died.

Mabel Wolfe, at least according to Sarah, was apparently not motivated enough by a sense of civic duty to tell the police everything she had seen. However, her daughter-in-law showing up, filled with anguish at her son's death and rage at Mabel for her incompetent guardianship, might have persuaded Grandma to spill the beans about what had happened. That could have led to Dr. Jim's death.

A more chilling thought crossed my mind. Had Eddie's mother included Mabel in her plan for revenge? I made a mental note to have Jack reconsider the possibility that Mabel's fall down the cellar stairs was no accident. In a mother's mind Mabel might be equally responsible for her son's death. But how could I find out the identity of this avenger?

I got up and walked across from the dining area to the living room. I looked out through the slider, across the marsh, to the ocean peeping above the row of houses lined up along the beach. Shadows were starting to fall. I checked my watch. It was already getting on to six-thirty.

Maybe Lauren was one of those lucky folks who'd had the advantage of growing up in a loving two-parent home, or at least had the benefit of a mother who had shown occasional interest in her. If so, she might have naturally considered the possibility that Eddie's mother would somehow be involved in the case.

Lauren had asked Sarah what was happening with the house. If it was on the market, Lauren could easily have gone through the listings and found the agent handling the place. A friendly conversation in which she suggested the possibility of having a potential buyer might have gotten her Edward Wolfe's address and phone number. After that, things got a little murkier.

If Lauren did call Edward Wolfe, she might have been able to persuade him to give her his ex-wife's name. But it would be harder to find out where she was living. Edward might not know, and even if the woman was living right here in Cornwall, she might not be easy to locate. I doubt she planned to put down roots in the town where she was going to commit a double homicide. She wouldn't even have a listed phone if she was just visiting. Hell, I only had an unlisted cell phone, aside from the yoga center number. Even if Edward did have a phone number for his wife and gave it to Lauren, I couldn't imagine Lauren giving the woman a ring and inviting her over to talk about her most recent murder.

I paused and warned myself I was getting way ahead of the evidence. What I had was a nice tissue of theories that explained most of what had happened, but it lacked any supporting structure in fact. One thing I could do was to call Edward Wolfe myself and find out if Lauren had gotten in touch with him. Jack would have his number in Mabel's accident report, but he was down in Boston, so a call would have to wait at least until tomorrow. I felt moderately satisfied. At least I had a theory to check, which put me way ahead of where I was yesterday.

CHAPTER 23

I grabbed my lightest fleece jacket and headed out the door. It was time to meet with Charlie. I'd been so busy thinking about the case, I had no idea what I was going to do about him.

As I drove toward the center of Cornwall, I reviewed the facts. He seemed to be getting along well with Julie, and they certainly taught a good class together. And from what I had seen, Charlie was proving to be popular, especially with the younger female clientele. But he was a self-confessed killer. I repeated that word to myself. "Killer" is a word that's sometimes equivalent to a condemnation, but there are lots of reasons to kill. If his father had been as violent as he said, his actions might have been justified. I'd certainly done my share of violent things that wouldn't look too nifty upon first glance, but I thought I could at least partially justify most of them. I wasn't looking forward to prying into Charlie's personal life or judging him. I knew how I'd feel about having someone probe into my innermost secrets.

I parked the car and walked across the parking lot to the yoga studio. I heard a car door open on my immediate right. A tall figure got out and turned toward me. Adrenaline began to pump, and I turned sideways, ready to fend off an attack. I relaxed when the person took another step and I saw it was Julie.

"Hi," she said.

I nodded. I didn't trust myself to say anything without betraying my jangled nerves.

"Charlie is going to be a little late. He got held up at work."
She stopped and bit her lip, revealing uncharacteristic nervousness. "I wanted to talk to you for a minute if you have the time."

I nodded again and moved toward the door. We didn't speak until we were upstairs and seated on the benches on opposite sides of the lobby. I smiled to myself at how often I seemed to end up in this room, sitting across from someone who disagreed with me.

"I know that you're planning to make a decision tonight about whether Charlie continues to work here," Julie began.

"We're just going to talk about some things."

"He's a good teacher, you know. A little shy, but who isn't when they first start out? He's a nice, gentle guy."

"I still have to ask him some questions."

"You mean about his past?"

"His past will probably come up."

"About the fact that he killed his father?"

I sighed. "What can I say, Julie? I'm responsible for the people I hire to teach. Even you have to admit that a guy who killed his father has some explaining to do."

Her pretty face frowned earnestly. "But his father used to beat his mother and abuse Charlie. Doesn't that make a difference?"

"It might, but I have to hear about it from Charlie. Maybe I even have to check up on the story to see if it's true."

Julie looked me in the eye, and for the first time her mask of politeness slipped. "Most people would say you have a lot more problems than Charlie does."

I smiled, which seemed to confuse Julie.

"They might be right," I admitted. "But that's the advantage of being the boss. I don't have to prove myself to anyone else. If people find me too weird, they just won't come to class, and I'll go out of business."

She got to her feet and looked down on me. "I want you to know that if you fire Charlie, I'm not going to teach here anymore."

I struggled to my feet, so I could look at her eye to eye.

"I'd be sorry to see you go. All I can promise you is that I will be as fair as I can in making my decision."

Julie waited for a moment, as if hoping I'd grant her more of a concession. When I didn't, she turned and walked down the stairs.

I went into the large front studio and turned on the floor lamps, which gave the room a warm glow adequate for class—just enough light to see what the instructor was demonstrating, but not enough to be distracting. I looked out through the window. In the distance I could see a few lights twinkling along the shoreline. Beyond the lights was the blackness of the sea. We live our lives trying to cling to a warm glow, knowing we are always on the edge of the universal darkness, I thought with a shiver. I sometimes envied those who had a faith that allowed them to believe the darkness was only temporary, a curtain concealing a large universe of light. Right or wrong, they were able to live their lives with a comfortable confidence denied to the rest of us, who stitched together a makeshift view of reality based on experience and reason.

I heard a noise behind me in the lobby and turned around, expecting to see Charlie. Instead it was Karen standing in the doorway of the studio. Her hands were behind her back, and she was watching me.

"Are you here to plead for Charlie as well?" I asked.

She gave me a puzzled frown.

"Sorry," I said. "Julie was just here trying to convince me to let Charlie stay on as a teacher."

"I've heard he's a good teacher," she said, walking toward me. "I've also heard that he killed his father."

"I'm surprised you know so much," I said.

Karen smiled. "Julie suggested he tell me because I'm so good at giving people helpful advice about their personal problems."

"That's probably because you have a degree in psychology."

She shook her head. "No. It's because I've spent so much time being treated by people in the field."

I felt a sudden shift under my feet as if someone had pulled the carpeting an inch or so while I was still standing on it. Loss of mental equilibrium often takes a physical form for me now. I shifted weight onto my good hip to compensate.

"I didn't know that."

"I didn't want you to. I didn't want anyone to know. Unfortunately, you were going to find out, sooner or later."

"Why do you say that?" I asked. "I don't do extensive background checks of all my employees."

Her left hand came out from behind her back in a sort of dismissive wave.

"No, of course you don't. Why should you? You wouldn't pass one yourself."

I took a step toward her. "I think this conversation has gone on long enough, Karen. Let's end it before you say something you can't take back."

Her left hand came up like that of a cop stopping traffic.

"You still don't understand, do you? I've been following you. I saw you go to Sarah Contell's this afternoon, and I know what she told you."

"Sarah told you what she said to me?"

Karen shook her head. "I know what she told Lauren, and I figure she told you the same thing."

I shifted my weight onto my good leg. I estimated the distance between us at ten feet. I could cover that quickly without overly straining my hip. I would ask Karen three more questions. As she was answering the third question I'd attack. When people are in the midst of framing a reply, they aren't as ready to defend themselves.

"When did you find that out?"

"You know when. The night Lauren died. She called to tell me she knew I was Eddie Wolfe's mother. After talking to Sarah, she called my ex-husband, and he told her my maiden name. I've been using that ever since the divorce. Lauren suggested we get together and talk about what I knew about Dr. Jim's disappearance."

"She didn't know you'd killed him?"

For the first time I saw surprise in Karen's face.

"How did you know I killed him?"

"His body was found. Even though you took him out into the ocean on a surfboard so he wouldn't drift into shore and people would think that he'd run off, it was your bad luck that he got picked up in a fishing net."

"How did you know about the surfboard?"

"An eyewitness can place you at the scene."

"I doubt that, or he'd have come forward before now."

I shrugged. "He saw you in the buff."

That seemed to bother Karen for a moment, but then she went on.

"Up until the last, when she finally lost consciousness, Lauren didn't believe I could kill someone. I was the sweet, motherly type who wanted to help people with their problems. She knew I was the blackmailer, but she fell all over herself telling me about how what Dr. Jim had done was terrible. And she didn't think my making him pay for his crimes had been so wrong. She thought all I'd taken from him was some money. As if money could ever repay what he did to me."

A darkness came into Karen's eyes. I thought it probably mirrored the red curtain that came down over my own mind before I gave way to my rage. Seeing myself from the outside made me realize how frightening I must be.

"So you killed Lauren," I said. I could feel my own anger starting to build. I should have asked my third question while I had more self-control because Karen saw something in my face. Her right hand came out from behind her back and I saw that it held a Taser.

"Stay where you are. This will drop you where you stand. It shoots up to fifteen feet and delivers two hundred thousand volts."

"Is that what you did to Dr. Jim?"

"I used a short-range stun gun on him. I knew he'd let me get close to him to hand me the money. From what Lauren has told me about him during the last two months, I knew he would never expect a woman to harm him. Once he was down, I taped a plastic bag around his head and waited for him to suffocate, then we took our little cruise out to sea."

"Is that what you're going to do to me?" I asked.

She shook her head. "Once you're unconscious, I think you'll have an accident on the stairs. Your bad hip will suddenly give out."

"There's no guarantee a fall will kill me."

Karen looked past me. "Those windows open, don't they? Maybe you decided to jump. Everyone knows you're only one step away from being suicidal. I know it's only three floors. With nothing but concrete below it should be enough. One thing I can guarantee is that you'll be going out head first."

"You don't exactly have the yogic approach to life. Why did you ever take a job here in the first place?"

"Because I'd learned yoga years ago. It was something I could do. I even taught it at one of the institutions I ended up in after my breakdown. I had enough money left over from the divorce to live without working for a while, but I wanted to fit into the community. I also wanted some way to meet the people who lived on the street where Eddie died."

A light went on in my mind. "You were the one who sent out the advertising leaflets for the yoga studio. You were only interested in the people who lived in Eddie's neighborhood."

Karen nodded. "My late mother-in-law, the incompetent drunk, could only tell me the car that hit Eddie was a dark color, driven by a man, and had MD plates. She kept whining about how she couldn't figure out a way to find out his identity and blackmail him. I checked the home address of every doctor in the area and found that none of them lived on her street. I called every doctor, pretending to do a newspaper article on what color cars doctors drove. Three of them had dark colored cars, but two were women and the other was a retired guy who hardly drove anymore. Finally, I figured that if I got to know some of the people who lived on the street, I might find out more about this doctor. You can imagine I couldn't believe my good luck when Lauren started telling me about her fiancé."

"So your mother-in-law did have useful information she could have given the police?"

"If she hadn't been so greedy and looking for a way to get more drinking money, she'd be alive today. When I heard what happened to Eddie, I took a little unauthorized leave from the institution where they were treating me. I was such a model citizen, no one expected me to try to escape. When I got down here, Mabel tried to tell me she didn't have any idea what had happened to Eddie. I convinced her she might lie to the police, but she shouldn't lie to me."

"Then you killed her?"

"Once Eddie died, her death was inevitable. She was as guilty of what happened to him as the doctor. She deserved to die. After I get through here, I'm going to visit my ex-husband and his girlfriend. They should never have abandoned Eddie."

The look in her eyes said with certainty there would be more deaths in the future.

I decided to push her buttons to see if I could force her into doing something stupid. I was also trying to calculate whether I could reach her before the electrodes reached me.

"But aren't you really the guilty one? If you hadn't ruined your marriage, Eddie would still be alive."

Her finger tightened on the Taser. I tensed, but then she smiled grimly. "And after all the others have paid, maybe it will be my turn. Sure, I'm guilty. And you, of all people, know what guilt feels like."

"What have I got to feel guilty about?"

"Maybe something you did in Iraq or something you didn't do. Whatever it was, I can see it written all over your face. I even feel a little bad about killing you because I think living is your punishment."

"You don't feel that bad. You tried to bash in my friend's skull the other night, thinking he was me."

"Mistaken identity. My apologies," she said with a grin.

"If I'm feeling so guilty, why don't you give me the Taser and let me put myself down?"

That brought a laugh, but there was something strange about it. It was more a silent stretching of the jaws, as if she wanted to consume something. I wondered how they had ever left her unrestrained in the institution she had come from, but then I remembered she had worked for me for two months, and I had seen her as a boring, bleeding heart rather than a dangerous killer. Like a lot of crazy people, she had great acting skills. Now she felt free to be herself.

"So you got to be friends with Lauren and Sarah, and pumped them for information about any doctors who might have been travelling on Eddie's street at night?"

"It was simple, really. Lauren was just waiting for a sympathetic ear to tell all her troubles to. I hardly had to ask any questions before I pretty much knew Jim Schianno had to have been the man who hit Eddie."

"You must have known all of this weeks ago. Why did you wait so long to act?"

"I had to plan it out. If he responded to the blackmail letter, I'd know he was definitely guilty. But I needed to have a way of getting rid of his body, so people wouldn't be sure he'd been murdered." She paused and gave me a smile that reminded me of the old Karen. "I really like living in Cornwall and working here. It's been one of the happiest times of my life. After your tragic death, I may buy the studio and reopen it myself."

"I thought you were planning to commit suicide."

She shrugged. "This way of life seems to have worked for you; maybe it would keep me going for a while longer, too."

The thought of Karen taking over my life tripped something in my mind. I could see the red curtain starting to move in from stage right. In a few more seconds I knew the animal part of my mind was going to act, no matter what the rest of my mind told it. It appeared suicidal to rush her while she held the Taser, but I might not get hit with a full charge, or my momentum could dislodge the electrodes enough to allow me to function. I could see Karen had read my mind because her hand tensed, and she was fully focused on me.

I heard a faint sound coming from the stairwell. I cleared my throat, hoping to conceal the noise from Karen. Keeping my eyes locked on hers, and twitching just enough to keep her focused on me, I let my peripheral vision bend around her until I could see Charlie walking across the lobby and standing in the doorway behind Karen. From where he stood, it looked like we were just having a conversation. I was about to tell Karen we had a visitor, so she should give it up. A Taser wouldn't do her much good against two. Before I could say anything, however, Charlie spoke.

"Hey, Ali, do you still want to see me tonight?"

Karen spun around with surprising speed. There was a buzzing sound and Charlie went down, twitching spasmodically on the floor. In two strides I was next to Karen, and I smashed the point of my elbow into the side of her head. That should have been enough to knock the average person unconscious, but Karen dropped to one knee and rolled away from me. An instant later she was back on her feet in a tae-kwon-do fighting position. She lashed out with a roundhouse kick that caught me high on my bad hip. I staggered back and just managed to avoid a second kick. She might have been short, but she was fast and strong. By keeping my bad left hip away from her, I was forced to be a southpaw, not a natural position for me.

She came in again. I faked a blow to her sternum with my right and caught her with a left to her chin. She took a step back, surprised and angry that she'd been hit. The next time she moved in, she switched to kicking with her left foot and caught me high on the shoulder. The kick was just a bluff, because she followed it up with a fist to my solar plexus. I blocked a little of it with my arm, but enough got through to take my breath away. I backed up, struggling to get my lungs to inflate. Unrelenting, she moved in again with a second kick to my bad hip. This one connected hard, and I hopped backward on one leg.

Sensing victory, Karen charged in with a series of kicks and punches. I caught most of the punches on my arms, and avoided the kicks by hopping away on my good leg. What Karen didn't know is that I'd had hours of practice using only my right leg while the hip was recovering. I can do almost everything most people can do on two legs with one.

As she came in again, I hopped to my left. I grabbed a handful of her hair and twisted her head around. I put my arm over her head, hoping to get a chokehold around her neck. I was just beginning to apply some pressure, when she twisted slightly. She brought up her right forearm and propelled the point of her elbow directly back into my nose. I felt the bone snap and a blinding pain brought tears to my eyes. For a moment I lost consciousness. Fortunately, I never lost my grip around Karen's neck or the fight would have been over. I could feel my lower face quickly covered with blood and mucus.

She was struggling for breath now, and I knew she must be seeing the stars that precede asphyxiation. Her arm came up again. I instinctively stepped back a bit to avoid another blow to my nose, and she took the opportunity to expertly flip me over her shoulder.

I did an awkward roll, and managed to make it to my feet. I glanced over my shoulder. Karen was coming toward me, but she was staggering slightly because her head still wasn't completely clear. I hip-hopped quickly across the room and out into the lobby, not daring to look back to see how close Karen was behind me. I had a baton in my desk drawer, if only I could reach it.

Before I got to my office door, a hard shove from behind spun me around; Karen charged forward, burying her head in my midriff. She began giving me hard body punches that crumpled me forward over her. She drove an upper cut to my chin that rocked me back on my heels and turned the world black. The Buddha clock on the table next to me began to bong out that it was seven forty-five. I didn't think I'd be around to hear eight.

With a last burst of effort, I brought my clasped together hands in front of me at waist level then drove upwards, catching Karen under the chin. It didn't hurt her much, but forced her to take a couple of steps back. With my right hand I grabbed the head of the Buddha who had just stopped ringing. Holding the large clock like a baseball bat, I swung forward as if going for a home run over the center field fence in Yankee Stadium. The heavy base of the clock connected with Karen's head and she went down.

I stood still for a moment, getting my senses back. Karen lay face down. I thought I should get her upright so she wouldn't suffocate, assuming she was still alive. I reached down and pulled her to her feet. She was completely limp. We leaned against each other side-by-side, the balancing of our weight holding us both erect.

I glanced up at the full-length mirror at the end of the lobby, and I saw clearly the difference between us.

I was taller.

There were footsteps on the stairs. A moment later Izzy's head appeared. He didn't say anything. The expression on his face said it all as he pulled out his cell phone and dialed 911. I heard him asking for an ambulance as I pushed Karen onto the bench. I sat down next to her, closed my eyes, and everything went black.

CHAPTER 24

I had the dream again. I've had it many times since I came home. I receive an official government notification that I am back in the Army and have been assigned to return to Iraq. At first I'm frightened and upset, and desperately trying to come up with some way to avoid going back. But I soon realize my return is inevitable. And as the time for my tour draws closer, I find myself becoming calmer, more resigned to my fate.

The dream usually skips to where I am now on the plane getting closer and closer to landing in Iraq. I stare out at the bleak, tan landscape below me and find myself looking forward to getting back.

In the next scene I'm in the mess tent back at my old base. Everyone is glad to see me. They come up and shake hands or hug me. Even those who have died, like Junior, are there to welcome me back. Then I see the captain. He smiles as he comes toward me, then opens his arms and gives me one of his powerful hugs. At that instant I know I am exactly where I belong. I know I should never have left, and no matter what happens to me in the future, this is the place I was meant to spend the rest of my life. I feel an emotion that is so strange to me, at first I don't recognize it for what it is.

I feel happy.

I opened my eyes, and the scene and the feeling of happiness disappeared. At first I thought that I must be outside in the snow because all I could see was white, then I raised my eyes and understood that the whiteness was coming from a large bandage covering my nose. I heard voices from somewhere outside of my field of vision. I craned my neck, ignoring the flash of pain in the back of my head. Over by the window, in what I slowly recognized as a hospital room, I saw Jack and Izzy in front of the window, talking softly like a couple of conspirators.

"What's going on here?" I tried to shout, but it came out as an indecipherable croak. But the croak got their attention, and they came scurrying over to stand next to my bed and stared at me like an exhibit in a sideshow.

"How do you feel?" Jack asked, giving the kind of forced smile reserved for people who look like death.

"I'm not sure," I answered honestly.

"The doctor was worried when you fainted. They thought you might have a concussion."

I nodded, then regretted it.

"They decided it was probably just the blood loss from your nose and the shot to the jaw you took catching up with you."

"How's Charlie?" I asked, starting to recall what happened.

"Fine," Jack says. "He was coming around by the time the police got there."

"He probably saved my life."

Jack nodded.

"I guess I owe him a job, regardless of what he did in the past."

Izzy had been standing there without speaking, so I glanced over at him.

"Your nose was badly broken," he says.

"Not the first time."

"Well, it was worse this time. The plastic surgeon said there was no point in trying to restore it to the way it was. He decided to completely restructure it," Izzy said ominously.

"What does that mean?"

"Well, he said it would be straight. In fact, he said once all the swelling and discoloration went away, you'd look beautiful."

I moaned.

"Sorry. I know that crooked nose was a badge of honor. But you'll get used to it. Being beautiful is nothing to be ashamed of."

I tried to glare at him, but the bandage got in the way.

"How's Karen?" I asked softly, for some reason dreading to hear that she was dead.

"She's got a bad concussion," Jack answered. "You really clocked her."

I ignored his feeble attempt at humor and thought that I'd really have to apologize to the Buddha for using him so violently.

"She'll live, then?"

"She'll live to faces charges of murder, I imagine, once we put the case together."

"Triple murder," I said, and gave a quick summary of what I'd learned.

"We're searching her apartment right now. We've already turned up another stun gun, a bottle of barbiturates identical to those in Lauren's system, and a draft copy of the letter she sent to Dr. Jim. I'm sure there will be more to come. We should be able to get her on at least a couple of the murders."

I closed my eyes and felt myself drifting off again.

Someone patted my arm. I opened my eyes and saw Izzy smiling.

"Get some rest. You'll be better soon and able to get back to your normal life."

"When was my life ever normal?" I said.

Izzy and Jack both smiled, but I caught them exchanging worried glances.

I closed my eyes. I hoped that if I closed them tightly enough I'd be able to return to my dream where I belonged.

ABOUT THE AUTHOR

Glen Ebisch has had over a dozen mysteries published for both young adults and adults. He lives with his wife in western Massachusetts. His interests include philosophy, Eastern religions, and yoga.